Smoky Hill Trail

Eighteen-year-old Jed Stone was a troubled young man. His family's home and land would be repossessed by the Denver Bank unless they made their next mortgage repayment. But there was no way the money could be found, unless by unlawful means.

His neighbours, the four McIver brothers, were in the same position and, against his will, Jed found himself planning a robbery with them. The McIvers got away with the strongbox but Jed was wounded and sentenced under an assumed name to five years in the Kansas Penitentiary.

On his release, two women came into his life as he returned home to get his share of the hold-up money. That was where the trouble would really begin!

Smoky Hill Trail

Mark Falcon

A Black Horse Western

ROBERT HALE · LONDON

ISBN-10: 0-7090-8168-5
ISBN-13: 978-0-7090-8168-5

Robert Hale Limited
Clerkenwell House
Clerkenwell Green
London EC1R 0HT

Typeset by
Derek Doyle & Associates, Shaw Heath
Printed and bound in Great Britain by
Antony Rowe Limited, Wiltshire

To Alan and Sylvia Tolman

CHAPTER ONE

Eighteen-year-old Jed Stone sat beside his parents facing the grey-bearded bank manager. Taylor Ramsay was not telling the family what they wanted to hear. They were in arrears with their mortgage repayments by three months and if some payment was not made by the end of the present month, the bank would foreclose on their mortgage and the Stones would lose their house and land.

Jed's spirits hit rock bottom and he knew his parents felt the same. He did not blame the bank. It was in business to make money, not lose it. Things had been hard for the family over the last year, as it had also been for his neighbours. There had been one disaster after another – first the plague of grasshoppers, then the drought, plus attacks from Indians. Some of Jed's neighbours had had their homes burnt out.

'I know things have been hard for you,' Taylor Ramsay was saying, bringing Jed back from his thoughts, 'but I'm afraid the bank can't allow any more credit. The end of the month,' he added with finality.

The Stones moved back their chairs and stood up in unison.

'We understand, Mr Ramsay,' John Stone answered for the family. 'I can't see any way of making up the shortfall in that time, but it'll give us time to settle our affairs. Jed and I will have to try and find work off the farm to pay off the arrears. Goodbye, Mr Ramsay, and thank you for being so understanding.'

Ramsay allowed a small smile to cross his thin lips. He was not a hard man, but he knew he had to do his duty by the bank. He stood up and shook hands with the family and ushered them out of his office.

Jed and his parents got up into the buckboard and left Denver for their home on Kiowa Creek, some fifty miles away along the Smoky Hill Trail. It was a quiet journey; the sadness and despair hung over them like a black cloud. Each of them had worked hard, back-breakingly hard, these past three years, clearing the ground, tilling the land and planting corn, only to be beaten by the elements, insects and Indians. They had borrowed from the bank to get started and after the first year they began to believe that things were going well. They were able to make their half-yearly payments on time to begin with but after the calamities all three of the Stones had almost lost the will to carry on.

Jed had seen his parents age before his eyes and this hurt him the most. How could he get some quick money to repay the bank? he wondered as he sat behind his parents in the buckboard. Rob a bank – or a stagecoach? Jed pursed his lips and shook his head at this thought. He'd never done anything dishonest in his life. He was hardly likely to start now. But the idea somehow would not leave his mind.

The next day was Saturday and after his usual chores Jed saddled up his horse and rode off back to Denver. If he raced his horse he reckoned he'd be there in five hours. It was one o'clock when he arrived.

He noticed the four McIver brothers entering the Gold Rush Saloon as he rode down the main street. They were his nearest neighbours and a rowdy lot. Jed did not entirely dislike them, but he knew they could never be his best friends.

Jed decided to join them. At least talking things over with someone else in the same position as himself, he felt it might somehow lighten his load.

The bar was quite full and the air was thick with smoke from hand-rolled cigarettes and cheroots. Jed spent most of his day in the open air and he immediately felt choked by the smoke-laden air and the close proximity of many men.

He walked up to the bar and ordered a beer, giving the McIver boys a curt nod.

'How are things?' Dooley McIver, the eldest of the four asked him.

'Could be a lot better,' was Jed's sombre reply.

'A sudden flow of money would help put things to rights, eh?' Dooley grinned, showing brown, tobacco-stained teeth. His brown, lank hair hung over his shoulders and Jed noticed the evil glint in his coal black eyes.

'You're so right, Dooley,' Jed replied. 'Got any ideas on the subject?'

Dooley looked slightly surprised and glanced quickly at his brothers.

'Have you been listenin' in on our conversation, Jed?' Dooley asked with another grin.

Jed furrowed his eyebrows. 'Why, have you been considering what I've been considering?'

'And what's that then, Jed?' Tam McIver asked him.

Jed's gaze shifted to the next eldest, a slightly smaller version of his elder brother, but his face was pock-marked.

'Holding up a bank or stagecoach.' Jed gave a short laugh. 'I'm not serious of course!' Jed added quickly.

'Let's discuss this out of earshot,' Dooley advised, taking hold of Jed's arm and leading him over to the corner table.

The McIver brothers followed, bringing their beers with them.

'Now listen here, boys,' Jed began, feeling slightly perturbed by the turn of events. 'I really wasn't being serious back there,' he added, pointing to the bar where they had just stood.

'Well *I* am,' Dooley declared. 'We're all in the same boat. The likes of us are never going to get the money to repay our debts by working the land. The gold around here is almost panned out, and all claims have been filed. We might just as well give up now as waste our time like we've been doing. Just one job and we'll be able to start afresh.'

Jed nodded. 'It sounds a good idea when you put it like that, Dooley. But it would never work. It wouldn't be honest.'

The brothers laughed at Jed's naïvety.

'Honest!' Dooley spat. 'Where does bein' honest get yer? Just one job, Jed. Then all our troubles'll be over.'

'Not scared, are you, Jed?' Brolin McIver cut in. 'Mebbe you ain't got the guts fer it?'

'I'd be a fool not to be scared of getting caught, Brolin,' Jed answered the even smaller McIver brother. 'I wouldn't want my folks to be ashamed of me.'

Hec McIver, the shortest, broadest of the brothers put forward his opinion of the idea.

'I reckon it takes guts to pull off a bank or stage-coach robbery. We've got guts, ain't we?' he demanded.

All eyes were upon Jed who suddenly felt trapped in the middle of a circle of hungry wolves. His manhood and bravery were in question. Did he want to show himself up as a coward, or would his conscience steer him on the right road?

'I don't know, fellers. It was only an idea that crossed my mind. I don't reckon I have got the guts to pull it off.'

Dooley's face was hard and deadly serious.

'Well that's too bad, Jed. You're in on it now. If we go ahead without you, you could inform on us for the reward. We can't have that. You're one of the McIver gang now, so let's start planning.'

Jed's stomach began to churn. He knew there was no way out for him now. He was well aware that if he refused to join them, his life would not be worth a dime. Men could die along the Smoky Hill Trail and who could prove who the killers were?

The McIver gang, as they now called themselves, arranged to meet up on the trail nearest their homesteads the following day and plan their next move. Jed felt deceitful as he lied to his father regarding his whereabouts. Jed had to admit to himself that it was a lame excuse he gave why he would not be accompanying him to the south pasture to help his father remove a stubborn tree stump.

'I said I'd help the McIvers at their place this morning, Pa. I'll come back and help you afterwards.'

'There are enough of them without any help from you, son. I need you more than they do.'

Jed noticed the disappointment in his father's eyes and felt guilty at his deception, but there was nothing he could do about it. He had already promised to be at the meeting place to plan the crime they were to commit.

'Sorry, Pa. I won't be long.' Jed jumped on his horse and rode swiftly away in the direction of Smoky Hill Trail.

The weekly stage left Denver the following day for Kansas City. There was likely to be a shipment of gold from the mines on board as well as passengers who could be relieved of any cash.

The gang decided on the spot where the coach would be held up. It was two hundred miles from the place they were at that moment on a bend in the road with cover from the hills. The coach would come upon them without any warning of the gang in wait.

'There's to be no killing,' Jed told them emphatically.

'Of course not!' Dooley grinned. 'We shouldn't get any trouble from anyone. We'll make a pact right now,' he said. 'When we've got the strongbox and any money the passengers might have, we ride like the devil towards town. If any one of us gets caught, he must make a vow not to inform on the rest of us. Is that clear?' Dooley demanded.

They all nodded.

'You in particular, Jed,' he added.

'I promise I won't give you away if anything happens to me, Dooley. There is one thing I'd like to add though,' he said, looking at each McIver brother in turn.

'What's that?' asked Tam, with interest.

'If I should get caught I want you to promise you'll take care of my folks with my share of the loot.'

'Why, naturally, Jed!' Dooley grinned. But Jed was not entirely convinced.

As they parted, the plans for the holdup now in place, Jed had a bad feeling at the pit of his stomach. He was not looking forward to what was to happen the following day. As he rode back home to help his father, a cold chill of foreboding passed through his body.

CHAPTER TWO

Jed had mounted up and left the house before his parents had woken up that fateful morning. How he wished he had not gotten involved with the McIvers. He had a premonition that something would go wrong with the hold-up and that he would not come out of it well.

As he reached Smoky Hill Trail and the place where he had arranged to meet the McIvers, he saw them already waiting for him.

'Glad you could make it, Jed,' said Dooley coldly. 'Where did you tell your folks you were going?'

'I didn't tell them anything. I left before they were awake.'

'Good,' Dooley nodded. 'The less they know about it, the better. Come on, let's get going!'

They rode for more than three hours. Dooley reckoned it would be better to hold the stage up over the border in Kansas than in Colorado and they needed to get there before the coach caught up with them. The horses would need a rest before they were ridden hard back to Colorado after the hold-up.

On the third day, Dooley called a halt at the first crossing of the south fork of Smoky Hill River. The plan was that the gang would keep under cover of the trees until they heard the coach coming and then take the driver and his cargo by surprise as the horses began to cross the river.

It seemed a long wait before at last they heard the approaching hoofs and the rattle of the coach approaching.

Jed found he was grinding his teeth with the tension.

'OK, cover your faces!' Dooley ordered.

The others did as they were told.

'Now!' Dooley said, and led the charge forward.

As feared, the coach had a shotgun guard on board who raised his rifle at the approach of the masked riders. Dooley fired at the man's hand before he pulled the trigger and the rifle dropped to the ground. Tam McIver already had the horses' reins in his hand as he pulled them to a halt.

'Throw down the box!' Dooley ordered. 'Then get down from there!'

Dan Johnson, the shotgun guard, was holding his bleeding hand with his other one.

16

'I'll need help with the box,' Johnson said, and stayed where he was.

'You – driver – get the goddamn box and throw it down! Then get down yourselves!'

Brolin had already relieved Curly Bill the driver of the rifle he was making an attempt to go for. He jerked his head and indicated with the held rifle for the two men to get down.

'All of you inside the coach, get out!' Dooley ordered, as he opened up the stagecoach door.

Five men and a woman did as they were told without any hesitation and stood before the masked men in obvious fear.

Tam had removed his hat and Dooley jerked his gun in its direction.

'I want all your money in that hat within the next two minutes. And I mean *all* your money. You, too, ma'am. Open up your little bag!'

The woman was middle-aged and very frightened. They could see her hands shake as she pulled the strings of her bag and opened it up. There were a few banknotes inside and a few dollars in coin.

'Much obliged, ma'am,' Dooley said amiably.

The hat was soon filled and Tam stuffed his pockets with the proceeds, then he put his hat back on.

While this was going on Jed sat astride his horse and did nothing.

Dooley tied a rope around the strongbox and remounted his horse.

'Let's get outa here!' Dooley ordered, dragging the strongbox behind him.

Jed had been mesmerized by the whole proceedings and it took him a second or two to comprehend that it was now all over and the gang were making their escape. Jed was the last to leave the scene and followed the others.

The sound of a shot rang out and Jed felt the bullet enter his back near his right shoulder-blade. The impact made him release his hold on his mount's reins and he felt himself falling from the saddle with a hefty thud on the ground. His horse continued at a gallop to follow the fleeing gang.

Curly Bill was the one who had shot at Jed's retreating back. The gang had taken the confiscated weapons with them but had missed another hidden in a compartment under the coach. Dan Johnson the shotgun guard was busy bandaging his injured hand with his neckerchief.

The rest of the gang did not stop to find out what had happened to Jed and the coach passengers. The driver and the shotgun guard were now standing by Jed's prone body. He was motionless and they thought that he was dead.

One of the passengers bent down and felt for a pulse on Jed's neck.

'He's still with us,' he told the rest of them.

'We'd better get him to a doctor.'

'Let him die, I say,' declared Curly Bill angrily. 'He don't deserve no doctoring.'

'But if we keep him alive, he can tell us who the rest of the gang are,' Johnson reminded him.

The driver nodded at the wisdom of this.

'What do we do now?' he asked. 'Do we carry on to Kansas City, or go back to Denver?'

'Go back, I reckon. The gang are more likely to come from Colorado and we're more likely to get some identification on this one' – he pointed to Jed, still lying on the ground – 'who'll tell us who the others are.'

'OK, Johnson,' the driver nodded.

'But there won't be another coach until next week!' one of the passengers exclaimed. 'I've got business in Kansas City which can't wait.'

Curly Bill gave a sigh as he thought it over.

'I've got my schedule to keep to,' he reminded Johnson. He jerked his head towards Jed. 'Help me put him into the coach! We're carrying on to Kansas City. We've left Colorado jurisdiction anyhow.'

'I don't know about the rest of you,' the woman began, 'but I want my money back and he's the only one who can tell us where it is. We'd better try and stop the bleeding before we start off. He'll be no good to us dead.'

'Hear hear!' said another passenger. He moved

19

towards Jed and took off his neckerchief to press into the bleeding wound. There was little more anyone could do for Jed at the moment. Dan Johnson had trouble of his own stopping the blood flow from his hand. Curly Bill and the passenger who had done the basic doctoring, helped Jed into the coach.

'That young girl Ellie Bryant at the next stage station will probably be able to patch him up a bit better than we can at the moment,' said Curly. 'She's had quite a bit of experience at doctoring on more than one occasion.'

Jed and the rest of the passengers were jolted along for the next twenty miles as the almost wild mustangs galloped at full speed to the stage station and a change of horses. This usually took only a couple of minutes but Jed's condition allowed the passengers a longer stop to stretch their legs and have some refreshment.

A slim, blonde-haired young woman of around Jed's own age greeted them at the door with a warm smile.

'We've got a couple of patients for you, Ellie, if you wouldn't mind,' Curly Bill informed her, as he and one of the passengers helped Jed inside the wooden building. A long table was in the centre of the room with a form on each side of it. Next to the table was a pot-bellied stove with something cooking in a large, black pot hanging over the embers on a hook. Around the walls were bunks for the passengers if the stage stopped for the night. Quite often though, the passengers were expected to get what sleep they could aboard the coach as it travelled through the night.

'Lay him face down on one of the bunks, Curly,' the girl Ellie told him. 'I'll see to him right away. Meanwhile, perhaps you'd all like to help yourself to stew from the pot, and coffee's hot too.'

Jed was barely conscious, but he was awake enough to notice the pretty young girl who was about to minister to his injury. Her blue eyes were bright and there was a slight smile on her lips. He tried to hold on to this picture as he was laid face down on a bunk.

'Help me get his shirt off,' she asked the woman passenger. The buttons had not been done up from the last time Jed had been looked at so it was comparatively easy to pull it off. Both women could not help but notice the muscular physique of the young man before them.

Ellie put some hot water in a small bowl and began bathing the wound with a clean cloth.

'Is the bullet still in there do you think?' Mrs Burton, the woman passenger asked her.

Ellie pulled Jed up slightly and saw the bullet hole at the front of his chest.

'Looks to me as if it went clear through, which is

a good thing in a way. Just so long as it doesn't get infected.'

'You're very young to be doing this,' Mrs Burton smiled.

Ellie returned the smile. 'You have to be able to do things like this around here, what with Indian attacks and the like.'

Mrs Burton looked at the young woman in admiration and helped her bandage Jed's cleaned wound with torn-up sheeting.

Between them they turned Jed over on to his back and propped his head up with a pillow.

'I bet he could do with some food inside him,' said Ellie, and brought him over a plate of stew.

'It's nothing special I'm afraid,' she told him, 'but we don't get the best of cuts from the company and we have to make do.'

'Thanks,' said Jed, and proceeded to eat heartily. He felt ravenous.

'What's the story?' Ellie asked Mrs Burton, as the woman sat down at the table.

'He and four others robbed the stage,' she answered. 'I must confess, though, that that one didn't do much. He just sat on his horse and watched the others. The driver shot him as he rode off. You'd better take a look at the guard's hand too, Ellie. One of the gang shot him before he could fire at them.'

Dan Johnson was eating at the table at that

moment and Ellie waited until he'd finished before she ministered to him also.

Ellie looked over towards Jed, who caught her eye mid-spoonful. He was a nice-looking fellow, thought Ellie. Jed flashed the girl a smile. She was a fine-looking woman. Pity he wouldn't get to know her better, he thought to himself.

CHAPTER THREE

The door of the stage post opened and a well-built, middle aged man entered.

'The coach is ready, folks. All aboard!'

Jed wondered if the man could be Ellie's father.

The passengers were given a couple more minutes to make use of the facilities – such as they were – and they boarded the coach drawn by fresh horses.

'We'd better tie this one up, I reckon,' said Curly to Dan Johnson, as he indicted Jed.

'He hasn't got a weapon, Curly. I don't think we'll get any trouble from him,' came the reply.

Curly nodded his bald pate. 'OK, Dan. I hope you're right.'

Joe Bryant, Ellie's father, held Jed by his right arm and assisted him into the coach.

'What's his name?' Joe asked Curly, as he was about to jump up into the driver's seat.

'He won't say,' said Curly. 'Can you tell the driver heading for Denver what happened and give his description to the law there? The other four got away with a strongbox and relieved the passengers of their money.'

'OK, Curly, I'll sure do that. Safe journey.'

By this time Curly and Dan were aboard the coach. The two gave Joe Bryant, Tom Bailey, his helper, and Ellie a wave of farewell.

It was a lonely life for the stage station employees, and Ellie especially looked forward to greeting the passengers to and from Kansas City and Denver. There was no time, however, to get to know any of them well, but Ellie asked numerous questions about life in places other than the station. Since her mother had died when she was ten, her only constant companion was her father. They had moved to the stage station two years before and had several battles with marauding Cheyenne and Arapaho braves after the horses. Ellie returned to the station house, but as usual, looked around her in the distance for any sign of movement. The building was well stocked with rifles and ammunition and the three at the station were always on their guard.

When the coach arrived in Kansas City, Jed was escorted by Dan and Curly to the sheriff's office and left in his charge. They then faced the stage company's manager in Kansas and explained the non-delivery of the gold shipment.

'A lot of good employing a shotgun guard!' John Pinder snarled when he heard the news. 'You're fired, Johnson. We'll find someone who's up to the job!'

Curly spoke up for his partner. 'Now hold on there, Mister Pinder. You can't do that! The gang were upon us before we knew it. Dan weren't to blame.'

'He should have been more alert. That's what we paid him for!'

Dan knew it was no use arguing with the manager. He would allow his hand to heal properly, then look for another job.

Curly explained that they had brought in one of the gang who Curly had shot while escaping, and was now with the sheriff.

'Who is he?' Pinder asked him.

'He wouldn't say. No doubt the sheriff will get it out of him. I reckon the gang came from Denver way. They headed off in that direction anyhow.'

'OK, here's your wages. Write me out a full report and have it on my desk by tonight. You'll be needed to give evidence at this man's trial, whenever that is. Goodbye!'

Curly and Dan exchanged glances. Writing out a report would be the hardest thing they had ever done – harder even than facing up to an armed gang of hold-up men. They each took a sheet of paper indicated to them by Pinder and left the office.

The tall, gaunt-looking sheriff stood over Jed as he lay on a bunk in a cell.

'My name's Sheriff George Riley. What's your name?' he demanded.

'I can't recall,' said Jed. The longer it took for them to find out who he was, the better. The McIvers would have longer to give an alibi for themselves and to hide the loot.

'Don't give me that!' Riley spat. 'Tell me your name . . .' he hesitated, '. . . or it will be the worse for you.'

Dan looked him straight in the eye but did not answer him.

'I need a doctor,' Jed informed him. 'I was shot in the shoulder.'

'Shame they didn't kill yer!' he exclaimed angrily. 'Tell me your name and I'll call for a doctor.'

Jed kept silent.

'OK, suit yourself,' Riley shrugged his broad shoulders.

'My name's Don Collins,' said Jed. 'Now get me a doctor!'

The sheriff looked squarely at him. 'How do I know you're not lying?'

'You don't. You wouldn't believe me whatever name I gave you anyhow,' he added.

Riley ground his teeth and shifted his weight between both feet. Jed expected to feel the man's fist at any moment.

'What are the names of the rest of the gang?' Riley asked him.

Jed pretended to think for a moment.

'I can't remember. I don't know them that well.'

Riley gave a growl of annoyance and left the cell, slamming the door behind him and locking it.

Jed was given neither water nor food until 7 o'clock that evening. His arm was giving him a lot of pain and there had been no sign of a doctor. Eventually, food, water and a doctor arrived almost together.

He had had plenty of time to think over the events of the last few days. His greatest concern was his parents who had no idea where he had gone. If they reported him missing to the law in Denver, then they would most likely put two and two together. When news got to Denver of the stage hold-up, they would be looking for Jed's accomplices. The McIvers were the family's nearest neighbours and they would be the first suspects.

Would the McIvers keep their promise and make sure Jed's parents were given money for the mortgage on their property? Jed wondered. He did not trust them but there was nothing he could do where he was. Would his sentence be a long one? Would he be hanged? Jed could only wait and see.

Dooley and his brothers rode like the wind for two miles, Dooley dragging the strongbox behind him.

At last they stopped and dismounted. The coach could either return to Denver, or keep going to its destination at Kansas City. The gang hoped the latter, which proved correct.

Dooley shot at the lock on the strongbox and was able to open the lid. As expected, the box contained bags of gold dust.

'How much is there?' Tom McIver asked.

Dooley took the bags out one by one, counting them as he did so.

'It's got one thousand dollars on each bag and there are fifteen bags, so how much is that, Tam?' Dooley grinned, trying to make his younger brother look stupid by not being able to count.

'Fifteen thousand!' Brolin exclaimed.for him.

'Dooley, if we show up with this amount of gold, everyone will know it was us who robbed the stage!'

'They sure will!' Dooley sighed. 'We'll use the cash we took from the passengers first, and then the gold a bit at a time so as not to raise any suspicion.'

The three brothers nodded at this suggestion.

'Where shall we hide it?' asked Hec, the youngest.

'Somewhere where we'll know where to find it again,' added Brolin.

There were numerous crevices in the rocks on the trail. They all realized that it would be no use putting a signpost next to the chosen place. It would need to be somewhere with a special feature they could remember.

'I reckon we'd better find a place nearer to home than this,' Tam put in.

'Yeah,' Dooley nodded. 'But not *too* close to home – and not on our own property either. When the law finds out who Jed Stone is and that he rode with four men, we'll be the first suspects.'

They put the bags of gold back into the strong-box and fastened it. Dooley tied the rope firmly around it and dragged it again as they set off once more towards home, keeping their eyes open for a likely spot to hide the box.

The next day they came to the south fork of the Republican River, crossed over and carried on. About half-way between the south fork and north fork, they spied a lone tree miraculously growing in a patch of earth in the rocks. The brothers looked at each other.

'What about near there?' Brolin pointed at the tree above them.

'We'll take a look,' said Dooley. They dismounted and the three younger brothers followed Dooley up the side of the hill.

'There's a hole at the back of the tree like it was made for the box,' Tam grinned.

'Go and fetch it, boys!' Dooley commanded, standing before the hiding place to wait for his orders to be carried out.

The box fitted snugly into the hole.

'Get some rocks to put in front of it!' said Dooley. The others did as he commanded without question.

The four brothers stood grinning broadly at each other thinking how clever they were.

'Come on, let's get home. Pa will be wondering where the hell we've been.'

CHAPTER FOUR

The day of the trial soon arrived. Jed had been interrogated mercilessly but he would not reveal the names of his accomplices. Neither would he give his real name, so he was tried under the name he had given – Don Collins.

If only he could get word to his parents what had happened to him, but maybe it was better for them not to know.

Jed was brought into the courtroom, his arms and ankles shackled, and he was forced to shuffle along to his place next to his lawyer, facing the judge's seat.

War had been declared between the North and South and the chatter from the spectators was more about that than the decision of Jed's fate, which would only be a formality.

Jed was brought forward to stand in the dock after the judge had seated himself comfortably.

The charge was read out and Jed was asked how he pleaded, to which he replied 'Guilty'. Again, he was asked who his accomplices were, and again Jed would not answer.

Jed noticed the shotgun guard and Curly, the coach driver. A pretty young girl sat next to Dan Johnson, the shotgun guard. Jed guessed they might be related. Johnson's arm was in a sling. Jed thought the man's hand ought to have been better by now. His own wound was almost healed.

Curly Bill and Dan Johnson described the hold-up, and explained that although Jed was present, he did not do anything except sit on his horse and watch.

Finally, the judge gave Jed five years hard labour. If he gave the names of the rest of the gang meanwhile, his sentence would be lessened. Jed served his full term. There was one small consolation, Jed did not have to fight his fellow Americans in the war.

The tall gates of the prison opened and Jed emerged. A prison wagon had delivered two prisoners to the prison and Jed was taken in the now empty wagon into Kansas City, some miles away.

An open carriage was waiting a few yards away from the prison gates, Jed noticed as he got into the wagon. A young woman sat behind the driver. She was holding a parasol which partly hid her face. Jed wondered what she could be doing there, but soon put her out of his mind.

The wagon moved off and within two hours he got out in the bustling town.

He did not need to ask the wagon driver where the stage depot was as it was prominently positioned in the main street close to where the wagon had stopped. The small amount of money Jed had in his pocket when he was jailed had been returned to him – enough to buy himself a ticket back to Denver.

There were five male passengers in the coach, including Jed. At the last minute a young woman was assisted into the coach by the driver, her carpetbag being tossed up on to the roof.

She settled herself between two of the male passengers. Jed wondered if she had been recently widowed as her clothes were black and a black veil covered her face. Jed sat opposite her and it was difficult not to keep looking at her. Although he did not realize it, this woman was the same one who sat in the carriage outside the prison. It was easier for her to look at Jed's face from behind the veil.

The coach waited a moment or two longer, but as no other passenger boarded, the frisky horses were eager to charge ahead on their journey.

'I hope we don't run into any injuns,' a small man with a bald head said.

'They've been on the war path down Colorado way since sixty-four,' a tall man added. 'You'da thought they'da learned their lesson after Sand Creek. There weren't too many left alive after that massacre.'

'Now the war's over there'll be more cavalry to keep them in line,' a broad-shouldered man in a corner seat added.

The same man looked at Jed. 'I suppose you did your duty in the war?' he asked him.

Jed did not answer. He was not proud of where he had spent the last five years.

'What line of work are you in, mister?' the bald-headed man asked Jed.

Jed looked the man full in the face as he answered.

'I worked for the government.'

There was a quizzical look on the small man's face.

'The government, eh? Secret work, was it?'

'I'm sworn to secrecy, so yes, it was secret work.'

The small man went on to tell the passengers almost all his life story. It passed the time, but Jed could tell that no one was really listening to him and after an hour of non-stop talking, the man was beginning to irritate them, Jed especially. He wanted some quiet time to think over what he was going to do with his life from now on.

Jed had served his sentence under the name of

Don Collins and had not written to his parents and of course had not received any letter from them. Were they still at their homestead? he wondered. Had they been able to keep up the mortgage? He doubted it. If they had been foreclosed, where were they now? If he did find them, would they want to see him again when they found out what he had done?

Then there were the McIvers. What had they done with the gold in the strongbox? Had they done as they had promised and given Jed's share of the robbery to them? If they had, Jed's parents would know that he had taken part in it. They would also know that the McIvers were the robbers and Jed had a nasty feeling that the McIvers would not want anyone to know this. Jed could not wait to get back home and find out what had happened in his absence.

At the eighth stage stop Jed got out of the coach with the others.

Jed had barely been conscious the last time he had travelled this way and each stop was the same to him. When he entered the room he was greeted by a pretty fair-haired, blue-eyed young woman of about Jed's age. He suddenly realized he had met her before and that she had tended to his shoulder. Jed's eyes lit up as recognition dawned on him.

The girl hardly gave him a look as she ushered

the passengers to the table where she ladled out stew. Jed sat down at the end of a bench. Five years had passed and the same thing was happening. The only difference was, he was no longer injured and was now able to take it all in. Jed wondered if the girl recognized him. She did not appear to. But then, she had met many different passengers in those five years and he realized it was hardly likely that she would remember any particular passenger.

The coaches often travelled through the night, but this time there was no relief driver and the one they had needed a few hours' sleep. It was therefore decided the passengers would stay the night at the relay station and make an early start in the morning.

There were bunks along the walls of the room for the passengers. As there was only one woman among them, Ellie suggested that she could sleep in her small room for more privacy, which the woman gratefully accepted.

Jed lay down on his hard bunk and would have dropped off to sleep except for the windbag named Ponsonby who was a medicine salesman – 'a remarkable remedy for every known illness' was his slogan. When the man eventually stopped talking he started snoring, loud enough to raise the roof. Jed had been used to sleeping in a room full of prisoners, many of whom snored, but this was just too much! Jed got out of his bunk and went outside. Sleeping out in the open would be better than this, he thought angrily to himself.

It was a clear night, the thousands of stars lighting up the sky were enough for him to make out his surroundings. A hay barn was to his left and Jed hoped a night in the hay would be more restful than in the stage station.

He opened the big barn door and peered inside, just making out the outline of harnesses hanging up and a ladder leading to the loft. He pulled the door closed and started up the ladder.

When he reached the top and stepped on to the loft floor he almost fell backwards as a voice came from out of the darkness before him.

'Who's there?' The voice was that of a female.

'Holy smoke!' Jed exclaimed, grabbing hold of a roof support before he fell backwards. 'Is that you, Miss Ellie?'

'It is,' she answered. 'Who are you?'

'My name's Je— Don Collins,' he replied, hoping she had not noticed that he was about to give his real name.

'What are you doing here?' she demanded.

'I'm sorry I disturbed you, miss, but I wanted some peace and quiet. That Ponsonby man was raising the roof with his snoring and I couldn't stand it any longer. I'll leave you in peace. Sorry,' he apologized again.

'It's OK,' she said. 'There's plenty of room for two up here.'

Jed was taken aback by this.

'I wouldn't want to lose you your good name, miss,' he replied.

'Oh I've already lost that!' she said. She gave a short laugh. 'Don't get me wrong. My 'good name' was taken from me – I didn't give it away.'

Jed did not know what to say.

'I remember you from years back,' she said. 'Didn't you rob a stage? I seem to recall tending to your shoulder. It was you, wasn't it?' she asked.

'It was me,' Jed confirmed. 'I didn't think you remembered.'

'I can't say that I'd thought about it – until now,' she added. 'I'd had other things to contend with.'

'Oh?' Jed prompted, sitting down some way from her.

'Are you sure you're interested?' she asked.

'If you want to tell me about it, I'm willing to listen.'

'OK, make yourself comfortable and I'll tell you about my adventures among the Indians. . . .'

CHAPTER FIVE

An Indian had been seen hanging around the stage station where Ellie Bryant and her father Joe worked, helped by Tom Bailey. He stayed just outside of gunshot range usually. Those at the stage station guessed he was after the horses, but he could have another reason for watching the place, Joe Bryant guessed: Ellie.

'Keep close to the house, Ellie,' her father warned. 'I wouldn't want him taking you off with him.'

Ellie smiled at this. 'What would he want with me, Pa? If he's looking for a wife, he'd choose someone of his own kind.'

A small smile crossed the man's gnarled features at his daughter's naïvety.

'He maybe wouldn't marry you, Ellie. But he might treat you as if you were married, if you see what I mean?'

Ellie looked into her father's face as it dawned on her what he was getting at. A shiver ran down her spine at the thought.

'I'll be careful, Pa,' she promised.

They didn't see the Indian for a couple of days and thought perhaps he had become tired of watching the place and they put him from their minds. If there were more than one of them they would have to worry.

It was while Ellie was putting out a line of washing that it happened. No one had seen the Indian and Ellie suddenly found herself lifted off her feet and pulled up in front of him on his horse. Within moments they were away and over the hill. Ellie had been too shocked to even utter a cry.

The brave's arms tightened around her waist as she came to her senses and started to struggle. He uttered a low growling noise which she supposed was a warning to keep still in his own language.

The horse pounded onwards and Ellie guessed that it must have been more than an hour before he pulled the animal to a halt and dismounted, dragging Ellie from its back. He held her closely to him and looked down at her beautiful face. He could tell she was afraid of him, yet there was defiance in her eyes as well as fear, which he admired.

As Ellie looked up into his black eyes she took in his facial features. She was surprised that, for an Indian, he was not at all bad looking. The arms that held her were muscular and Ellie felt a strange, unknown feeling pass through her body. What would he do to her? she wondered.

He did not attempt to be intimate with her and allowed her to rest for a while before they set off again. She knew she would not get away from him so it was useless to even try. He lifted her up on to his mount's back and sprang up behind her and they were off at a gallop again towards his village.

When they arrived they were surrounded by all the members of his tribe. He jumped easily to the ground and pulled her down roughly from the horse.

Several braves spoke to him in the Cheyenne tongue and Ellie didn't know what they said, but they were laughing and looking at her, so she knew they were talking about her.

'So you've got yourself a squaw at last, Eagle,' one of them said. 'Wouldn't any of the village girls have you so you had to steal a white woman?'

'She appealed to me. She is different,' Eagle explained.

'You're going to have trouble with her, Eagle,' one called after him as he gripped Ellie's wrist and pulled her towards one of the tepees.

An old woman was sitting in the tepee, sewing some moccasins.

'What have we here, son?' the woman said as they entered.

42

'This is my woman, Mother,' Eagle replied. 'She will give me many fine sons.'

'A girl from your own tribe would give you better ones,' the old woman said.

'Find her some proper clothes, Mother. She can stay here with you until our marriage. The woman must be hungry.'

'Do you even know her name, son?' she asked.

'No. I will give her a Cheyenne name.' Eagle looked at Ellie and thought for a moment. 'Her name will be Golden Hair.'

The old woman nodded in agreement. 'It is a suitable name. I will instruct her in the Cheyenne way. When will be your marriage?'

'Find out when she will be fertile. I will marry her then.'

Eagle pulled the flap aside and left the tepee. A moment later a young woman entered and spoke to the old woman. Later Ellie found out that Morning Song was Eagle's sister, who also lived in the tepee. Eagle's father had been killed by soldiers two years before.

It was difficult at first for Ellie to understand what the two women were saying to her, but by gestures and repeated words, Ellie soon came to know certain words. The women pulled off her clothes and they examined the white-skinned young woman before them. They seemed satisfied with what they saw, for Ellie was indeed a fine-looking woman and shapely too. A white doe-skin dress was provided and they slipped it over her head. It reached just above her knees. Ellie wished she had a long mirror so she could see what she looked like.

Eagle's mother, White Dove, indicated that she sit down on the floor of the tepee. A small fire was burning in the centre of the place with a big pot hanging over the embers. White Dove ladled out some food into a wooden bowl and handed it to her. Ellie was not given a spoon and soon realized she would have to drink the liquid from the bowl and eat the meat and roots with her fingers. It was a strange taste, one that Ellie had never tasted before, but it was edible and as she started eating, she realized how hungry she was.

During the afternoon Eagle entered the tepee.

'How is she behaving, Mother?' he asked in the Cheyenne tongue.

'She is giving us no trouble, son, but her capture will cause trouble with the White Man.'

'We have other captives in the village. The White Man would rather buy them back than fight for them.'

White Dove shook her head slowly. She was not convinced.

Eagle took Ellie's hand and pulled her to her feet. She was forced to follow him outside. They walked together until they came to the largest tepee in the village.

'Black Kettle!' Eagle called.

An old man pulled back the flap on the tepee and came out. He was nothing special to look at, Ellie thought, but there was an air of authority about him. Could this be their chief? she wondered.

'Ah, Eagle, my nephew. So this is your captive! You will make good trade for her.'

Eagle shook his head. 'No, Uncle,' Eagle replied. 'I intend her to be my wife. I will not trade her – unless she proves to be unsuitable.'

Within a month Eagle took Ellie for his wife and set up home together in Eagle's own tepee next to his mother and sister. He had treated her with respect and kindness and gradually Ellie's feelings for her husband grew. Soon there was new life within her womb.

Gold had been found in Colorado which brought in more than 50,000 eager prospectors by 1859. The intruders on Indian land caused resentfulness and hostilities and rumours of an Indian war were rife. Major-General Samuel R. Curtis, army commander of the Kansas and Colorado department wanted any pretext to drive the Indians out. Colonel John Chivington was also an Indian-hater. He had once been a Methodist preacher until he led the Union to victory at Glorieta Pass. He now commanded the district of Colorado.

On 7 April 1864 Chivington reported to Curtis that the Cheyenne had raided 175 cattle from a ranch on the Smoky Hill Trail. Although this proved to be untrue it did not stop Governor John Evans from giving him an order to burn villages and kill all Cheyenne he found.

Ellie often thought of her father back at the stage station, but she found herself becoming more like a real Indian every day. She felt safe and happy until one day word came to the camp that four Cheyenne villages had been razed and Chief Lean Bear, a peaceful Cheyenne, had been shot, despite walking up to the white man proudly wearing a medal the Great Father in Washington had given him. Arapahoes and some Kiowa tried to intercede in the dispute but were also fired upon. Now the Cheyenne and Arapaho in Colorado were on the warpath.

A family was murdered at a ranch outside Denver and the corpses were taken to Denver and displayed. Traffic on the trails were attacked by Arapaho and Cheyenne and Denver was virtually cut off. During three weeks in August fifty people were killed. Ellie's husband, Eagle, came into the village one day after a hunting trip and told the gathered villagers how he had witnessed four white men shooting dead a white man and woman outside their home off the Smoky Hill Trail. At this piece of information, Jed's heart seemed to stop beating for a second. His own parents lived there – or at least they were living there when he last saw them five years ago. Could it possibly be them who had been killed?

'The Indian has been blamed for many things. The killing of these two white people will be blamed on them, too,' Eagle said.

In the September of 1864, Ellie gave birth to a fine son who was named Little Wolf. She could see her husband was well pleased and proud of his offspring. She was helped by her mother-in-law, White Dove, with her delivery and afterwards.

The Cheyenne, Kiowas, Commanches, Arapahoes, Apaches and Sioux were unaware that the War Department had authorized Governor Evans to raise a special regiment of Indian-fighting volunteers who would serve for one hundred days. The 3rd Colorado Regiment – 'the Hundred Dazers' – was mustered under the command of Colonel Chivington, 'the Fighting Parson', but around the same time peace suddenly broke out. Major Edward W. Wynkoop at Fort Lyon was contacted by representatives of the warring tribes. He visited Black Kettle at his village.

Ellie noticed that four captives were released and guessed this was part of a bargain Black Kettle had agreed to. The old chief agreed that his tribe would settle at Fort Lyon and would be protected by Major Wynkoop, but Wynkoop was hastily replaced by Major Scott J. Anthony. Protecting the surrendered Cheyenne and Arapaho was furthest from his mind. He had the village moved to an almost dry watercourse about forty miles to the north-east called Sand Creek.

CHAPTER SIX

As Jed lay there in the hay loft he could tell that Ellie's voice had changed. It no longer sounded confident and matter-of-fact. Her words faltered and seemed to stick in her throat. It was obvious to him that what she was about to convey was going to be hard for her. He felt like crawling over to her and taking her in his arms to comfort her, but he didn't. It would seem like he was taking advantage of her feelings when she was at her most vulnerable.

'You don't have to continue if you don't want to, Miss Ellie,' Jed told her.

'I must,' she said. 'I haven't told a soul about it since I came back here – not even my father.'

She cleared her throat and continued with her story. Jed guessed she needed to as a way of releasing her demons.

*

It was daybreak on a clear frosty morning of 29 November 1964. Black Kettle's village was quiet, only the bark of a dog sounded as it sensed riders were approaching.

Ellie heard it and she sat up in the warm buffalo robe. Her son made a small cry and she realized he was hungry. As she proceeded to breast feed him she heard sounds outside. Something was wrong.

Ellie put on her dress and went to the tepee opening and pulled back the flap. There were many soldiers approaching and they looked far from friendly.

'Kill and scalp all, big and little; nits make lice,' roared Chivington.

'But Major, they've made peace!' a junior officer protested.

'I have come to kill Indians, and believe that it is right and honourable to use any means under God's heaven to kill Indians!' Chivington waved his sabre in the air and the 700 soldiers advanced on Black Kettle's camp.

The Indians didn't stand a chance. Most of them were still asleep and were cut down or shot in their tents. Black Kettle did not understand what was happening and ran up the Stars and Stripes outside his tent, followed by a white flag of surrender. Still the carnage continued.

Ellie picked up her son and went outside. If they

saw she was a white woman, surely they would stop the killing?

A small child was standing outside one of the tepees, crying for its mother and was used as target practice. The soldiers jeered and laughed as the child fell dead.

'No!' Ellie cried, as loud as her voice would let her. 'Stop it! Stop it!'

The soldiers who had just killed the child rode up to her and Ellie's heart was pounding within her breast. Their eyes were wild and insane and Ellie felt very afraid.

'We've got a captive here, boys!' one of them said as he reached her.

'Is that your baby, lady?' one of them asked, looking down at her from his horse.

'Yes. Why are you doing this? Black Kettle made peace with the white man.'

'Major Chivington's orders,' the same soldier replied, at the same time leaning down and grabbing Ellie's baby.

'Where's its father?' he asked her.

'He's away, hunting.'

'Check inside,' he told one of the men, indicating Ellie's tepee.

'No one here,' he answered.

'Give me back my baby!' Ellie screamed.

The man already held his sabre. He threw the baby into the air and the tiny infant fell on to the upturned blade, which went right through him. The soldier pulled the blade free of the baby and tossed him on to the ground. It was obvious he was dead.

Ellie's screams rent the air and she went down on her knees to pick up the lifeless, bloody body, holding it to her chest.

'I've done you a good turn, lady. When you get back into decent, civilized society, you'll be accepted easier without a stinking Indian brat.'

Decent, civilized society.

If this was an example of *decent civilized society* then Ellie wanted nothing to do with it. The Indians she had lived with over the past months were far more decent and civilized than these unholy monsters.

Ellie was shaking uncontrollably and she cradled her dead baby in her arms as if doing so would bring him back to life.

The soldiers moved on, chasing running Indians and cutting them down. There were not many men in the camp. They had gone with Eagle to bring back food for the village. They had few weapons as they had surrendered most of them to Major Wynkoop when the peace treaty was signed.

Many atrocities were carried out on the bodies, cutting out the women's private parts and breasts, and taking scalps.

This could not possibly be happening. Surely

Ellie was having a dreadful nightmare and she would wake up soon to find everything was quiet and normal in the village.

At last the carnage was over. Everywhere was quiet. Ellie later learned that 28 men and 105 women and children were slaughtered. Among those who escaped was Black Kettle who had carried his badly injured wife on his back.

Ellie was taken to Fort Lyon with two other captives and later she was escorted back to her home at the stage station from where she was abducted.

CHAPTER SEVEN

Ellie finished telling her story and both she and Jed were silent for a few minutes.

At last Jed said, 'I'm really sorry, Miss Ellie. I don't know what else to say.'

Ellie did not answer.

'And you say you haven't even told your father all you have gone through – not even that you had a baby – a son?'

'No,' she replied with a catch in her voice. 'I didn't speak a word for over a month. I couldn't speak, 'though I tried. I'm not sure how my pa would react if he knew I'd had a baby by an Indian. He'd probably disown me.'

'Surely not!' Jed exclaimed. 'None of it was your fault. I feel' – he hesitated – 'kinda honoured that you told it all to me. Maybe now you'll start to feel a lot better and can begin to get on with your life again?'

'Maybe you're right,' she sighed. 'I won't keep you awake any longer. Goodnight.'

'Goodnight, Ellie.' Jed rolled on his side and thought over all that Ellie had told him. It seemed only a few moments later that the early light of morning came through the cracks in the barn walls. He called to Ellie, but there was no answer. He began to realize that she was no longer there and must have gone back to the stage station some time before.

Jed was the last to sit down at the table for breakfast. He felt the other passengers' eyes on him and guessed they knew that he had not spent the night in the same room as them. He hoped he had not compromised Ellie.

She came up to him last of all after giving the others their breakfast which consisted of belly pork and beans with a slice of bread, washed down with a cup of coffee. Their eyes met for the briefest of seconds but she moved on as though she had never spent the night in the hayloft with him.

'Our company wasn't good enough for you last night, sir?' Ponsonby stated rather than asked Jed.

'I found it too noisy,' Jed replied.

'And Miss Ellie – you too found it noisy in here?' Ponsonby looked up into Ellie's eyes.

Ellie ignored his question and gave a plate of food to her father and his helper. She could tell the driver was eager to be off and he had been served first.

Jed was able to see the woman passenger's face clearly now that she had pulled her veil back over her head. She was an attractive young woman and could be no more than about eighteen, Jed guessed.

Soon the passengers were ready to climb aboard the coach which was ready for them outside. The horses were restless and eager to get going once more.

Jed held back while the others boarded and stopped at Ellie's side.

'Are you likely to be back this way again?' she asked.

'Would you like it if I did come back, Ellie?'

She noticed that he had called her Ellie this time and not Miss Ellie.

'I must confess I would very much like to see you again,' she told him.

Jed smiled down at her. 'I've got some business to attend to Denver way. I'm not sure how it will all turn out, but if everything goes well, I'd like to come back for you – if you'd have me.'

Ellie smiled up at him and nodded.

'Ellie' – he hesitated – 'what if meanwhile your man, Eagle, comes back for you? Would you go with him?'

She looked down at the ground and Jed could

tell she was finding it difficult to answer.

'I had some feelings for him, I admit it, but it would be too hard to go back. I'm a white woman, not an Indian.'

They were interrupted by the driver. 'The coach is waiting, mister! We haven't got all day!'

Jed quickly took Ellie's hands in his.

'Goodbye – for now, Ellie. I hope to be back again quite soon.'

'Goodbye . . . I don't even know your name.'

'I'll tell you next time we meet.'

Jed jumped aboard the coach and closed the door behind him. He waved at Ellie as the coach sped off into the distance.

After two more days of travel, the coach and its passengers entered Denver. The place was bustling.

Jed had no gun and no horse. He also had very little money. What he had in his pockets when he was arrested in Kansas was returned to him and there was enough to hire a horse for his journey back home – if indeed it was still his home. His gun had not been returned to him and he felt ill at ease at the thought of riding without a weapon. It occurred to him that if he was accosted by more than one man then a gun would not be of much use to him.

Jed noticed that the young woman dressed in

black was making her way to the hotel. He also noticed that she looked back at him a time or two. There was something strange about her that Jed could not fathom out.

It was around ten in the morning. Jed looked at the money he had on him and reckoned he could buy himself a meal and coffee before hiring himself a horse to take him home.

Half an hour later Jed rode out of town. A slightly built young man came out of the hotel and stepped on to the boardwalk. He saw that Jed was leaving town. He hurried to the livery stable and was soon riding in the same direction. There was just enough gap between them for the young man to follow without being noticed, or so he hoped.

Within two hours Jed had reached Kiowa Creek, the turn off from Smoky Hill Trail. Soon he would be home – or would it still be his home? he wondered.

Jed stopped for a few seconds and looked around him. Everywhere was quiet, except for the sound of a horse's hoofs. The rider urged his mount behind some rocks, but he had not been quick enough. Jed had seen him. Who was he? Jed wondered. Was he a detective, following him to find out who Jed's accomplices were and where the money or gold was that was in the strongbox the McIvers had ridden off with? As Jed had no means of defending himself, he decided to pretend he did not know he was being followed.

Jed rode on until he came to his home. It looked the same as he'd left it. Were his parents inside, or was it occupied by someone else?

Jed dismounted and threw the horse's reins over the hitching rail outside the door. He knocked. It felt strange knocking on his own door, but if indeed his parents were inside, they would be startled by someone just opening the door and walking in.

Jed heard footsteps coming to the door. His heartbeats began to quicken slightly in anticipation. At last the door opened. The man before him was holding a gun in his hand. Jed looked up from the gun to the man's face. It was the eldest McIver brother, Dooley. There was surprise and shock on the man's face at seeing Jed standing there.

'Where are my mom and pa?' Jed asked directly. 'What are you doing here?'

'Come on in, Jed!' Dooley smiled, revealing his tobacco-stained teeth.

'You can put that gun away first,' Jed told him curtly.

'Sure thing!' he answered.

The other three McIver brothers came up to them and Jed noticed that they did not look pleased to see him. What was going on? Jed wondered. Where were his parents? Had they left the place and moved elsewhere?

Suddenly, Jed had a terrible thought. When Ellie had told him her story of her life with the Cheyenne, her husband had told her of four men who had killed a man and woman at a place off the Smoky Hill Trail. And they had been white men, not Indians.

'Where are my parents, Dooley?' Jed asked the oldest brother.

'Sit down, Jed. I've got some bad news for you.'

Jed sat down in a familiar armchair and waited for Dooley to continue.

'Your ma and pa were killed by filthy Indians – Cheyenne I think they were. We saw them do it and chased them off.'

Jed looked up into Dooley's coal black eyes and knew the man was lying.

CHAPTER EIGHT

'I'd like to ask you fellers one question,' Jed began.

'Fire away, Jed,' Dooley answered, a false friendly smile on his face.

'Why are you boys living in my house?'

Dooley gave a short laugh.

'We're takin' care of it for you – for when you came outa prison.'

'That's real kind of you. What about your own place?'

'Oh, we go back there now and then.'

There was something about their attitude that was worrying Jed. They feigned friendship, but the hairs bristling at the back of his neck warned him these men were not his friends.

'Well, now I'm back, you can go back to your own home. Thanks for taking care of the place for me.'

Dooley pursed his lips and shifted the weight on

to his other foot.

'Well now, the thing is, Jed, you don't own this place no more. We bought you out. We bought out the Hungates as well. Injuns got them, too. We took them into town to show the townsfolk what them Injuns did to them. It caused quite a stir. Riled them up it did, what with them and then your folks. The military made them Cheyenne and Arapaho pay for what they'd done at a place called Sand Creek.'

The Hungate family. Jed had heard of them, but he had never met them before. He was sure the McIvers were responsible for his parents' deaths, but could they have killed the Hungates too? He feared he would never know for sure.

Jed was uncertain how to proceed from here. There were four of them and he hadn't got a gun. If he got on their wrong side, he felt sure they would not hesitate in putting him out of the way for good. Most likely they would blame it on the Indians also.

'I served five years in prison for you boys. Paying off the mortgage on this place is only a small percentage of the amount you owe me from that strongbox.'

'Yeah, I suppose it's only fittin' that we cut you in. The trouble is, we stashed it in a hiding place miles from here. We haven't used it all at once, so as not to arouse suspicion, if you see what I mean.'

Tam McIver looked up quickly at the window. He had seen something move outside and was out of the door in a second, his gun in his hand.

'What's wrong, Tam?' Dooley asked.

'Someone's out there. Someone followed you here, Jed,' said Tam.

The others pulled out their guns and went to the door. Tam inched his way around the building, going left. Dooley and the others went right.

'Drop your gun, mister!' Jed heard Dooley order.

A few seconds later a slightly built young man with a droopy moustache covering his top lip preceded the four McIver brothers into the house.

'Have you seen this feller before, Jed?' Dooley asked him.

'No. Never,' he replied, but at the back of his mind he had a feeling that this was not the first time they had met.

'What are you doing skulking around here?' Dooley demanded of the young man.

He did not reply.

'I asked you a question, mister. What do you want?'

The voice, when it came, was low and husky.

'I was looking for someone. I was told he lived around here along Kiowa Creek.'

'Who were you looking for?' Jed asked him.

'A man named Don Collins,' he replied.

63

'No one of that name lives around here,' Brolin McIver told him. 'What shall we do with him, Dooley. Is he a spy do you reckon?'

As Jed looked hard at the young man's face, it occurred to him that his moustache was growing at a lopsided angle, as if a false one had been stuck on to the top of his lip. A small smile came to Jed's lips as he realized who this 'man' was. The young woman passenger from Kansas who had been dressed in black with a veil over her face for the most part. Who could she be working for? Jed wondered. A detective agency employed by Wells Fargo? It was risky letting a woman ride on his trail. What on earth was he to do now? He couldn't let the McIvers kill her, but how was he going to prevent it without a gun? He also had his own life to think about.

To take the McIvers' minds off the newcomer, Jed said, 'How about something to eat, boys? I'm famished.' This was not strictly true as Jed had already eaten before he left Denver.

'Hec, see what we've got and we'll all eat,' Dooley told his youngest brother.

As Hec turned to do Dooley's bidding, Dooley returned to the young 'man' before him.

'Come on, out with it! What are you doing snooping around here?'

'I told you,' he replied. 'I'm after a man called Don Collins.' As the pretender spoke 'his' eyes

64

were on Jed. He knew the youngster was aware of Jed's assumed name.

'And I told you, there's no one of that name in these parts. What do you want him for anyways?'

The young 'man' shook his head. 'I'm not prepared to say. I'll leave now and look elsewhere.'

'Oh no you don't! Sit down there while we think what to do with you. There's something mighty strange about you,' Dooley snarled.

Just as the young man reluctantly sat down at the table there came a mighty thump on the door.

All present looked at each other.

'What the hell was that?' Dooley asked of them all.

Within a few seconds the smell of smoke came to their nostrils. They all knew what the noise had been.

Brolin ran to the window and looked towards the door.

'A fire arrow!' he yelled. 'Boys, we've got company!'

Dooley grabbed a rifle and gingerly opened the door just enough to be able to use the rifle to knock the arrow from the door which was already starting to burn. Another arrow thwacked in its place, then another. There was a bloodthirsty yell from outside. They were being rushed while the door was open.

The brothers grabbed up their rifles and two

bodies fell almost simultaneously before they entered the cabin. Dooley slammed the door shut before another dark-skinned brave could enter.

The sound of other fire arrows were heard from the roof. They were going to be burnt alive.

Tam and Dooley smashed the window and fired at the approaching warriors. The smell of smoke was getting thicker by the minute.

Jed looked down at the young woman posing as a man as she sat at the table. He could tell she was afraid, but was hiding it bravely. Jed didn't know why the girl was trailing him, but he had a feeling she wanted him to lead her to the McIvers who had been his accomplices in the stage hold-up. And that is precisely what he had done. Jed had kept his part of the bargain and had served time for all of them, but they had certainly not kept theirs. Not only had they not taken care of his parents, but also he was sure it had not been Indians who had killed them. As far as Jed was concerned the McIvers could die. But he had no intention of dying himself, and would do all he could to save the girl. The trouble was, how?

'Dooley, give me a gun – and give him his gun back, too!' Jed demanded.

Dooley nodded over towards Hec who had not had time to start preparing any food. He threw the young woman's gun over to her and found one for Jed.

'Save a bullet for yourself,' Jed told her.

She gave a nod, but at the same time began to tremble.

The Indians also had guns and a bullet whizzed through the glassless window, finding its mark in Tam.

Dooley swore and returned the fire, again and again, until the trigger fell on an empty chamber.

'More shells!' Dooley yelled at anyone who could provide some.

A box of cartridges came towards him through the air and Dooley and Brolin fumbled in their haste to reload, dropping some of the shells on the floor.

A fire arrow came through the window and lodged in the table only a few inches from where the girl sat.

Jed banged the flames out with the butt of his gun, burning his hand in the process. The girl grabbed a ladle of water from a bucket and poured it over Jed's hand. Their eyes met.

'Thanks,' he smiled.

A gasp came from the window as Dooley was hit between the eyes.

'Dooley!' Brolin and Hec yelled simultaneously.

There was nothing they could do for their brother. There was only the two of them left now.

'Jed, get over here by the window!' Brolin yelled.

Jed moved towards the window to take Dooley's place.

'Come here by me!' he told the woman. 'You're in direct line of fire where you are.'

She hurried to his side and her face brushed his arm. She hardly knew this man, but somehow she felt safe being near him.

Brolin bobbed up to take a shot at an approaching Indian but a bullet found its mark in his chest. Now there was only Hec left of the McIvers.

Jed fired at and killed another Indian. He tried to see how many there were out there. He knew they couldn't last much longer.

Then Hec was hit in the stomach. The bullet didn't kill the youngest McIver outright and Jed winced as he knew the pain the young man was in. Hec screamed and yelled and then whimpered like a baby. The woman crawled over towards him to see if she could do anything to help, but by the amount of blood oozing out of the wound, she knew he didn't have long to last.

'Before you go, Hec, is any of the gold left from the hold-up?' Jed called across the room to the remaining McIver. He realized he must have sounded callous, but he had to know before it was too late.

'Yes,' Hec whispered.

'Where is it then?' Jed demanded.

'Lone ... tree.' His voice came out almost inaudibly.

'Where?' Jed demanded, and quickly fired off

another shot outside.

'Along . . . Smoky . . . Hill . . . Trail.' A rasping sound came from somewhere in the man's chest and his head slumped forward.

'He's gone,' the woman said.

Now only the man she knew as Don Collins and herself remained. And the cabin was burning – burning too much to be put out.

CHAPTER NINE

'Mr Collins!' the woman's voice was almost hysterical. 'What can we do?'

'Start praying, lady,' Jed replied. 'And while you're at it, there's a trapdoor under the rug beneath the table. Pull it up and get down there, quick!'

Jed made sure she was doing what she had been told, then shot the next Indian about to push through the door. He quickly followed the retreating figure and pulled down the trapdoor behind him. The rug was nailed to the door and no one would know there was a hiding place beneath it.

The woman fell the remaining steps down and Jed stumbled into her when he reached the floor of the cellar. It was pitch dark but the cracks that were in the floor boards above them let in some smoke.

'Mr Collins, we'll be smoked out even if we

aren't burnt out,' the woman almost wailed in the darkness.

'Keep quiet or they'll know we're still alive. Hold my hand and follow me!' he ordered.

She not only held his hand, she held on to his arm also. She did not ask where they were going as she had been told to keep quiet.

Jed felt his way across the small room below the cabin and came up to the hole in a corner.

'You'll have to crawl from now on,' he whispered. 'Follow me!'

She did, and found herself trying to keep her face away from his retreating heels.

It seemed an eternity to her, but in actual fact they had been crawling on hands and knees for only five minutes. She wanted to ask him how much further they would have to go, but decided against it. She was in his hands and if he had wanted to do her any harm, he would have done it by now.

Jed could see a small chink of light ahead of him and he knew they were away from the cabin. He felt sure that once the cabin had completely burnt down, the Indians would lose interest and move off. He only hoped that they would leave the horses, but somehow he doubted that. It would be a mightly long walk back to Denver.

Jed reached the slit of light and pushed upwards, very slowly and carefully. His eyes became accustomed to the light outside and he looked in all the directions he was able to see. The Indians were moving off. He couldn't see any of the horses being led away, but they might already have gone. He waited . . . and waited.

The woman grew impatient.

'What's going on?' she whispered.

'They're moving off,' he replied, equally quietly. 'We'll wait a while until we're sure it's clear, then we'll get out of here.'

'My heart's still beating fast,' she admitted.

He smiled in the darkness. It felt good being her protector, although they were not out of danger yet.

The light was fading outside their bolt-hole. Jed could just make out the last embers from the burnt-out cabin some distance away. He still could not see any horses.

At last Jed decided it was time to leave.

'Come on,' he told her, 'let's start walking.'

She followed him out of the dark hole and Jed lowered the door back after them. He scattered some soil and vegetation over it.

'I don't know why I'm doing this,' he said. 'I don't intend coming back here. But if the Indians return, they won't know we escaped.'

'You didn't seem sorry when those men in the cabin died,' she remarked.

'That's because I wasn't. They killed my parents

and blamed it on the Indians.'

He noticed the sharp intake of breath beside him.

'How do you know that for sure?' she asked him.

'Because someone saw them do it. An Indian to be precise. It's a long story – one I've had trouble getting my head around – but you're right. I was glad when the McIvers were killed – especially by the Indians. It was right and just that the Indians killed them. The McIvers were probably part of the cause of the Indian wars around here. The army needed some excuse for the Sand Creek massacre, but this didn't stop the fighting, it only stirred up the tribes into taking revenge.'

'You seem to know a lot about it, Mr Collins. Were you involved with it all?'

He gave a short laugh. 'Hardly. I was penned up in Kansas prison at the time.'

'Of course,' she replied.

He looked sideways at her as they began walking towards Smoky Hill Trail.

'Who are you, anyway?' he demanded. 'You're sure as hell not a man.'

She did not reply immediately and Jed continued, 'You're that woman from the stage, aren't you? You were dressed all in black with a veil over your face. You know something about the hold-up I was involved in, don't you?'

'That's right,' she answered. 'You served your

time for the robbery, but the others didn't, and one of them shot my father – the stagecoach guard.

Jed frowned as he tried to remember what had happened on that fateful day.

'He was shot in the hand if I recall,' he said. 'I don't remember much about it as I was shot from my horse and things were a bit hazy after that.'

'I know from the passengers, the driver and my father that you didn't have much to do with the robbery, but I wanted you to lead me to the others.'

Jed shook his head in slight bewilderment.

'Just because your father got shot in the hand?' he asked incredulously.

'It must seem only a small thing to you, Mr Collins, but my father's hand got infected and he had to have it amputated. After that it was difficult for him to find work. He got depressed and' – she hesitated and Jed noticed the catch in her voice – 'and he drank himself to death. My mother and I had a hard time of it after that.'

Jed was silent. He could quite understand how things would have been for a woman and her daughter left alone to fend for themselves.

'I'm real sorry, miss,' said Jed, and by his tone, the girl knew he was sincere.

'Are you after the gold now, or was it only justice you wanted for your father?' he asked her.

'I've just seen justice, Mr Collins, so I might as well get my hands on some compensation. We didn't get any from the Stage Company.'

Jed nodded in the darkness and noted the bitterness in her voice. 'I can't say that I blame you, miss. I reckon I've paid for what's left of it – five years of payment. If we do find it, we'll share it – half each. Agree?'

'I suppose so. But it's not ours to share though, is it?'

Jed tutted. 'You're not going all sanctimonious on me now, are you?'

The girl grinned. 'No. We've got to find it first though.'

They continued walking for an hour, keeping to the well-worn trail beside Kiowa Creek. There were several groups of cattle along the way, no doubt bought with the ill-gotten gains from the hold-up by the McIvers.

'I reckon we'd better rest up a while, miss,' Jed suggested. 'We've got a long way to go before we even reach Smoky Hill Trail.'

She sat down almost immediately beside a rock without any argument. She was hoping this man beside her would suggest it quite soon.

Jed lay a foot or two away from her. The last woman he had spent the night with was Ellie. Her beautiful face came to him and he wondered how she was. He hoped the station hadn't been invaded by Indians. He couldn't bear the thought of her being killed or abducted again. Jed knew she had seemed quite eager for him to return to her. He wondered if it would happen at some time in the future.

Jed was awake first the next morning at first light. The woman saw that he was kneeling down by the creek and taking some water with his two cupped hands. He was conscious of her moving behind him and he looked back at her.

'The water's good,' he said. 'Come and drink some, then we'll be off again.'

She did as he advised and within a few minutes they were walking along again towards the trail that led to Denver.

With constant rests, they finally reached Smoky Hill Trail. Jed looked up at the sun and guessed it was around midday. He looked across at the woman by his side and smiled.

'If you want people to believe you're a man, you'd better fix that moustache: it's crooked.'

Her hand went straight to the false moustache under her nose and adjusted it, pushing it down hard so it would stay on.

'Is that better?' she asked.

He nodded. 'I guess so, but you'd look a whole lot better to me without it.' He gave a short laugh and she joined in.

'I wonder if I've been missed at the hotel. I signed in, changed into these clothes and left. I hope they've kept my room for me.'

Jed nodded. 'I hope so, too. Maybe they've sent out a search party for you?'

They carried on walking. It hadn't seemed half so far from Smoky Hill Trail to the cabin the day before, the woman was thinking to herself. But she was riding a horse then, which would make some difference.

'I don't know your name,' Jed remarked, hoping she would supply it.

'Lily,' she said. 'Lily Johnson.'

Jed felt her looking at him and she eventually asked the question she had been wanting to ask for some time.

'Is your name really Don Collins?'

'Nope,' he replied. 'My real name's Jed Stone, but I didn't want my folks to find out that I was a thief – even if the money was to pay for the mortgage that was overdue.'

Lily nodded. 'I see.'

Jed wondered if she really did, but let it pass.

They finally reached Smoky Hill Trail and the turning left led to Denver. Jed wondered what would happen next. He had hired the horse which was taken by the Indians, he had only a few coins in his pocket – not even enough for a bed for the night – and definitely not enough to buy a horse to take him to the lone tree that Hec McIver had told him about. Things were looking pretty bleak.

CHAPTER TEN

Jed could tell that Lily was finding the long walk hard as her steps were getting slower. Eventually she came to a complete stop.

'I've had it,' she announced, and promptly sat down on the ground.

'You've done pretty well,' Jed told her. 'I wanted to call a halt way back but you kept going so I did, too.'

She removed her hat, allowing her dark hair to fall over her shoulders. She looked comical now with long hair and a moustache.

'I dare say you've had it hard these past years?' she said. 'What did you do – break rocks and such like?'

Jed nodded. 'Yeah, a pretty useless occupation. A complete waste of time. It did give me muscles I never had before though,' he smiled slightly.

'Kinda like going in a boy and coming out a man?'

He nodded again. 'It made a man of me, that's for sure!' he exclaimed. 'There's always a top dog in every prison. If he's eaten his own food and wants some more, then he just takes it from the nearest one to him who's got some left. It was a case of either keeping well away from him or fighting back. I sure learnt to fight in there, but only after being beaten up pretty bad first.'

Lily's mouth was open as she pictured what had happened to Jed in prison.

'When you decided to follow me, what was your intention, Lily? Were you going to kill me and the McIvers? You could hardly have arrested us on your own.'

Lily shrugged her shoulders and raised an eyebrow.

'I was pretty stupid, huh?' she grinned.

'That's one word for it,' Jed replied. 'Those McIvers would have ended up killing you, you know – me too, no doubt about it!'

'Saved by the Indians then, weren't we?'

'Yeah, and by the trapdoor my pa put in the cabin for such an eventuality.'

The sound of pounding hoofs came from behind them and Jed looked back down the trail.

'Put your hat back on and cover up your hair, Lily! There's a stage approaching. We might get ourselves a ride back to Denver.'

Within a few minutes the stage was almost upon

them and Jed stepped into the centre of the trail
and held up his arms and waved.

'They'll think they're being held up!' Lily said.

They were almost run over as the driver had
difficulty bringing the horses to a halt from a pace
similar to a stampede.

'Whoa! Whoa!' the driver yelled at the half-
tamed mustangs.

'We've been burnt out by Indians and our
horses taken. Can you give us a ride into town?' Jed
asked.

'Those goddamn Indians! They've been busy.
The last stage post was attacked and burnt out and
they took the change of horses. These have gone
for more'n forty miles without a break. There's
room for one inside and another on top,' the stage
driver told him.

The man's words made Jed's heart freeze with
alarm. It must have been the same stage post
where Ellie lived.

'You go inside, and I'll go on top,' Jed told Lily.

When Jed was settled and the stage began the
last part of its journey to Denver, Jed called to the
driver.

'Were they all killed at the stage post?'

'We found the bodies of three men with arrows in
them and their scalps taken,' was his bitter answer.

'No sign of a golden-haired woman – Ellie was
her name?'

'No. She was either inside the building or . . .' he hesitated, fearing to complete his sentence.'

'You mean she could've been taken off with them?'

'That's most likely what happened.' He nodded. 'You knew Ellie Bryant?' he asked.

'Yeah. If she was taken off, I hope it was by a brave called Eagle. He took her for his wife and they had a son together. The baby was killed at Sand Creek and Ellie was returned to her father at the station.'

'It might have been better if she had been killed,' was the driver's opinion.

Jed's mind was in turmoil. He had wanted to find the rest of the hold-up money and take Ellie away with him and start life afresh, but now . . .

Ellie's face came into his mind once more. Whatever had happened to her, he knew it would take a long time before he would forget her. What if he tracked her down and bought her freedom? Would the Indians agree to it? Would Ellie want to leave her man?

Eventually the stage rolled into Denver and stopped outside the hotel. Jed jumped down and thanked the driver for the ride and met Lily getting out of the coach.

'Now I've got to get into my room without being recognized,' she whispered. 'I think you'd better follow me after a few minutes. My room number is five.'

Jed waited outside and looked through the open door as Lily made her way up the stairs. The hotel clerk had his back to her at that moment. When she had reached the top of the stairs, Jed entered and followed her up. Her door was open and he knocked before entering.

'I'll change back into a woman and then we'll get something to eat,' she said, a suggestion Jed wholeheartedly agreed with.

'The thing is' – Jed hesitated – 'I'm broke.'

'I'm not so well off myself,' Lily grinned. 'I've enough to pay the hotel bill and buy us some food though.'

'What about enough for two horses?' he asked hopefully.

'How much do you reckon horses cost?'

Jed shrugged. 'Forty dollars – each, maybe.'

Lily winced. 'I'll have to have a look in my purse.'

Jed waited while she pulled out some dollar bills and counted them.

'You've got a fair bit of money there, Lily,' Jed commented.

Her dark eyes flashed up to him.

'It's not much for nearly five years hard work,' she replied. 'My mother and I took in dressmaking after my father couldn't find work.'

'What about your mother? Is she still alive?' he asked.

83

She shook her head, and Jed thought he detected a tear in her eyes.

'She died two weeks before I set out to follow you. I found out when your release date was and I wanted to get even.'

'That's why you wore black with a veil over your face?'

She nodded again.

'Do you think we'll find any gold, Jed? Perhaps the McIvers spent it all by now.'

'That thought had crossed my mind more than once,' he replied. 'We might be going on a wild goose chase – *and* we might meet up with more Indians along the trail. Do you still want to carry on, Lily?'

'Yes I do,' she said emphatically. 'If I don't, I'll always regret not looking, no matter what happens to me.'

Jed laid on Lily's bed while she washed and changed into a dress behind a screen.

'Mm, that feels better!' she said. Jed did not answer so she took a peek around the side of the screen. Jed was fast asleep. Lily smiled. It seemed a shame to wake him so she sat in a chair and waited.

Half an hour later she woke up to find Jed sitting on the edge of the bed with a smile on his face.

Lily looked startled.

'I only meant to close my eyes for a few

moments. Have I slept for long?'

'No idea,' he said. 'I was asleep myself for a while. Shall we get some food now? You'll have to pay, though,' he added.

'All right. You can pay me back from your share of the gold we find.'

As Jed sat opposite Lily at a table in the dining-room, he realized this was the first time he had really seen her face. It had been covered by a veil on the way to Denver, and later it had a moustache added until they reached her hotel room. He had to admit that she was a fine-looking young woman.

As they got talking, Jed told her what the coach driver had said on their way to Denver.

'They found the men at the stage station killed and scalped, but there was no sign of Ellie.'

'She was the woman who let me use her room at the stage station?'

Jed nodded. 'That night I couldn't sleep with the noise that man Ponsonby was making, so I went up into the hay loft. Ellie was there – but I didn't know that at the time,' he added hastily.

Jed told Lily Ellie's story and finished with, 'I'm going back there to make sure she wasn't inside the station house when it was burnt out. If there aren't any . . . remains . . . I'm gonna find her. Her husband, Eagle, probably snatched her back.'

'Jed!' Lily exclaimed. 'You can't! They'll kill you!'

'I've gotta do it, Lily. I'll never rest easy until I find her.'

Lily's face was crestfallen.

'You can't have fallen in love with her in so short a time. Please don't do it, I beg of you!'

CHAPTER ELEVEN

Jed chewed on a mouthful of food and looked at the young woman before him.

'Why are you so much against me finding Ellie?' he asked. 'I should have thought your only reason for tagging along with me is to find the gold. Once you've got it, you've no more need of me.'

'A few days ago I would have agreed with you,' she answered. 'Now . . .' She shrugged. 'You've become part of my life.'

Jed continued chewing, trying to find a suitable answer.

'Remember, Jed, you need me to pay for the horses to get us where we're heading.'

'I am aware of that,' he said abruptly. 'That don't mean we've got to be tied together forever.'

Lily lowered her eyes and felt as if he'd struck her across her face.

'No,' she replied softly. 'Of course not.'

They finished their meal in silence and Jed stood up.

'Do I book myself a room, or am I sharing yours?' he asked her. He felt uncomfortable being beholden to her for everything.

She did not answer right away and continued looking down at her empty plate. She had never intended it to be the way it had turned out, but she realized they both needed one another for different reasons. She needed him for his protection and he needed her to finance the operation.

'As we'll be spending the days – and nights – together, there hardly seems much point in being prudish about sharing a room. A room, mind, *not* a bed,' she emphasized.

'The thought had never entered my mind,' Jed smiled.

She caught the twinkle in his grey eyes and found herself returning the smile.

Jed spent the night on Lily's bedroom floor. He was used to sleeping on bare boards with only a blanket to cover him over the past five years, so it came as no hardship to him.

Lily undressed behind the screen and put on a white cotten nightdress. Her dark hair flowed over her shoulders and Jed caught his breath at the sight of her. This woman before him was beautiful.

She got into bed and blew out the lamp.

'Goodnight, Jed,' she said.

'Goodnight, Lily. Sleep well.'

Unbeknown to either of them, they both lay awake in the darkness, unable to sleep, deeply aware of the other's presence in the room. At last sleep claimed them and it did not seem long before morning. They were soon dressed and ready for breakfast.

Jed left the hotel first, and Lily followed him after paying for her room.

They met at the livery stables and Jed was already bargaining with the livery owner over the price of two horses. The man reminded Jed that he had not returned his mount after hiring it.

Lily came up to them and explained they had both lost the horses to Indians who had burnt out their home.

'That's hardly my fault, ma'am,' he told her. 'You'll have to pay for the first two horses as well.'

Jed looked at Lily. Would she have enough on her to pay for four horses?

Lily put her carpetbag down and opened up her purse. She turned away from them as she counted out the money. It left her with only a few dollars.

'Here,' she said, holding out the money.

'Thank you, ma'am. You're paying for his mounts too?' he asked, looking from one to the other.

'Yes, my . . . brother lost his money in the fire.'

Jed's eyebrows shot up at her unexpected words.

He guessed she was trying to save his face with her explanation at paying for them both.

'Anyhow,' the stable owner began, 'I rented the other horse out to a man, not you.'

Lily looked flustered, hastily searching for some explanation.

'He was my other brother,' she lied. 'He . . . he was killed by Indians.'

The stable owner searched her eyes and noted the look of sadness in them.

'I'm sure sorry to hear that, ma'am. Mebbe I can knock some off the price in the circumstances. Them darn Indians!' he growled. 'You would have thought that Sand Creek would have put a stop to all these raids!'

'Seems to me,' Jed interjected, 'the Sand Creek Massacre was the *start* of the raids.'

'How can you be an Indian-lover after what they did to your family?' the livery man asked.

'Who said I was an Indian-lover?' Jed snarled. 'I met someone who was there. It wasn't pretty by all accounts. Women, children and tiny babies were slaughtered. Most of the men were away hunting and the rest couldn't defend themselves. They had already given up most of their weapons.'

The other man looked sceptical.

'That's not how it was told to us. Colonel Chivington's men said it was a hard battle, but the soldiers won.'

Jed's lips were set in a firm line. He shook his head, unwilling to argue the point.

'I'll return twenty dollars, ma'am. I can't make it any more.'

Lily took it from him and returned it to her purse.

'Much obliged, mister,' she said.

'Come on, Lily, let's get outa here!' Jed told her, taking hold of his mount's reins.

He helped her into the saddle and handed her up her carpetbag.

'I think mebbe you should have worn something more suitable for riding,' he said as he mounted up.

'I could hardly have paid for my room dressed as a man, could I?' she snapped.

'Mm, I suppose not,' said Jed. 'Have you got your riding clothes in that bag?' he indicated with his head.

'Yes. I'll change when we get out of town. How far have we got to go to where you and the McIvers held up the stage?'

'Around 150 miles I reckon.'

'We won't get there in one day then?' said Lily.

'It'll probably take about two days, depending on how fast we ride. Stop off at the general store,' said Jed.

'What for?' asked Lily. What else was she going to have to pay for? she wondered.

'We'll need food and canteens for water – also a couple of bedrolls.'

Lily went quiet. She would have to spend more than one night out in the open with Jed, she realized. And then what? If they did find the hidden gold what would happen next? Where would they go? She had nowhere and no one to go back to. If Jed did as he said he would, and go in search of Ellie, she would be completely alone. An involuntary shiver went through her body.

Lily's constant presence had made Jed forget Ellie at times, but her face would come into his mind when he was not expecting it. If only he knew her fate. He wanted to find her again, no matter how dangerous it would be for him. He knew he would most probably be killed – and not in a quick way either.

Also there was Lily to think of. He somehow felt responsible for her safety. He had not asked her to join him, but he couldn't just abandon her.

Outside the store, Lily handed him the twenty dollars the stable owner had returned to her.

Jed took it and their eyes met. He realized that if he had not met Lily he would have had no money to get him to the gold. Did she think he was taking her for granted? he wondered.

He came back to her after a few minutes and tied the gunny sack containing food on to the saddle horn together with a canteen of water, and then fixed his bedroll on to the cantle. He handed Lily a canteen and attached the other bedroll to her horse's saddle cantle.

They left Denver and when they had reached the fork in the trail leading to Jed's old homestead, Lily dismounted and changed into the trousers and shirt she had worn before. She did not fix the false moustache above her top lip this time, and allowed her hair to fall loosely down her back.

Jed watched her fold her dress into a tight bundle so it would fit into her bag more easily. Her change of clothes was quite a transformation, but now, without the moustache, she was still a beautiful woman.

They continued to ride along Smoky Hill Trail at an easy trot so as not to tire the horses and stopped at midday for a break. Lily felt stiff. She had never ridden so far in her life before and she hoped she could keep going.

After a while Lily said what had been on her mind for some time.

'Jed, why don't we stop at one of the relay stations? They'd give us a meal and we could rest up.'

'They wouldn't *give* us a meal, Lily. They'd charge us for it. When we get our hands on that gold, then we can have all the comfort we can buy.'

Lily nodded. What Jed had said was quite true,

and she decided not to suggest anything like it again.

Jed noted her expression change at his words and felt a little sorry for her.

'Don't forget,' he added, 'they'll want to know why we're riding the trail instead of going by coach. After all, there's nothing out here that anyone would want to head for, and we wouldn't want to tell them what we're doing – would we?' he finished with a smile.

'You're quite right,' she nodded. 'I didn't think of that.'

'Until we get hold of that gold, it's best that no one knows what we're up to. I don't want to end up back in prison – and I wouldn't want you to go there, either.'

She nodded again and their eyes met. If anyone had told her a while ago that she would be riding the trail with an ex-convict, and going after the gold he had stolen, she would never have believed it. But here she was, riding by his side. She realized at that moment that she liked the man. She liked him a lot. She sighed inwardly as she remembered that Ellie was the only woman on Jed's mind.

CHAPTER TWELVE

Jed and Lily took about a half-hour break after every fifteen to twenty miles. By the time the light was fading Jed reckoned they had travelled seventy-five miles that day. Both had kept their eyes open for a lone tree growing beside the trail, but so far neither had seen one. It would take about another half a day before they reached the south fork of the Smoky Hill River, which was where Jed and the McIvers had held up the coach. It occurred to Jed that his partners in crime would not have hidden the gold too far away from their home on Kiowa Creek. They had obviously used quite a proportion of it to buy his homestead, enabling them to join Jed's place with theirs. Then there was the herd of cows they had also bought. Could there be much left by now – if any? he wondered.

Jed unsaddled the horses and used the bridles in

a figure of eight to hobble the horses' front legs so they did not wander off too far in the night.

Lily noticed that he placed the bedrolls with some distance between them. She would have preferred to be nearer to him in the dark.

Jed produced some jerky from the gunny sack and handed it to her.

'Is that all?' Lily asked with a frown.

' 'Fraid so,' he answered. 'You'll get used to it. I've been used to worse at times over the past five years.'

'You must think I'm always grumbling,' she said.

'Not really. It must be a bit hard for you. Just think of the rewards you'll get when we find the gold.'

She grinned. 'That thought does help a bit,' she admitted.

They settled down to sleep that night. The sky was filled with stars and a gentle breeze was blowing on their cheeks. The mournful call of the whippoorwill came to their ears and there seemed to be rustles now and again. Lily shivered as she wondered what kind of animals they could be. At last she could bear it no longer.

'Jed, I'm scared of the dark!'

A smile came to Jed's lips.

'There's more to be afraid of in daylight,' he told her. 'Two-legged varmints. That sort won't bother us in the dark,' he assured her.

'Are you sure, Jed?' came her frightened little voice.

'*Almost* quite sure,' he laughed.

They were silent, then, 'Jed?'

'Yes.'

'Would you mind if I came closer to you? I wouldn't be so afraid then.'

'Sure,' he agreed.

Jed felt her bring her bedroll right up close to him. He wasn't sure it was such a good idea as the closeness of her would send him crazy. He thought of Ellie again.

As if she was reading his mind, Lily asked, 'Jed . . . did you . . . make love to Ellie in the hay barn?'

The silence seemed long to Lily as she waited for a reply. As it did not come immediately she realized she had no right to ask the question. It was none of her business. It was not as if she and Jed were engaged to be married. He had made it perfectly clear to her that she was only with him to finance the trip.

'I'm sorry, Jed,' she said at last. 'I had no right to ask that.'

'Mebbe not,' he said quietly. 'But the answer, if you're so interested is, no. We spent most of the night talking – or rather Ellie did most of the talking – I just listened. When I woke up the next morning she'd left and was serving out breakfast when I went back to the station.'

'Oh,' Lily nodded to herself in the darkness, and a big smile crossed her lips. 'Goodnight, Jed.'

Jed smiled to himself. 'Goodnight, Lily.'

He did not fall asleep immediately, but thought over the last few days. He had not been alone except for a while when he rode out to his home and met up again with the McIvers. He had not had the chance to grieve for his parents. Five years had been a big chunk out of his life and he almost forgot what they had looked like. Just their outlines came into his mind, not their faces.

At last he drifted off and slept soundly until morning.

Lily was walking around and bending her knees up as if in a little war dance. Jed realized she was stiff through lack of exercise.

After tearing off a couple of mouthfuls of jerky, followed by some water from their canteens, they were mounted up again. The horses had wandered a short way in search of grass during the night, but the hobbles had kept them near for easy saddling.

At around four 'o'clock that afternoon they came upon the south fork of Smoky Hill River. Jed stopped abruptly and Lily noticed the frown on his forehead.

'What's wrong, Jed?' asked Lily.

'This is where we held up the coach,' he explained as he dismounted to allow his horse to drink from the creek.

'So?' asked Lily.

'So, we've missed the lone tree Hec told us about before he croaked. *If* there was a lone tree. I'm having serious doubts about it. Mebbe it was his idea of a joke, to have the last laugh on us before he went.'

'Oh no!' Lily exclaimed. 'What'll we do now, Jed?'

Jed felt completely deflated and was at a loss to know what to do after their long journey.

At last he said, 'We'll go back and look harder.'

Jed remounted and set his horse at a canter. Lily followed behind, but would have preferred to stop for a break.

After another hour Lily's voice came to him from behind.

'Jed. I want to stop for a while!'

He half turned his head.

'Can't you hold on a bit longer?' he called.

'I could,' she answered, 'but I reckon you'd better come back here. I think I've found that lone tree.'

Jed pulled his horse around at once and cantered back to her.

Lily had dismounted and was holding her horse's reins.

'Look!' she pointed. 'You were in such a darned hurry, you missed this small . . . canyon I suppose you'd call it.'

Jed's mouth opened as he looked at the horse-shoe shaped inlet in the rocks – with a stunted tree at the 'toe' end of it.

They exchanged looks, their eyes brightening in anticipation.

Lily ran with her horse and Jed rode up to the tree and dismounted.

He looked all around the roots sticking out of the rocky ground, hoping to find some sign of disturbance where a stongbox could have been buried. Lily noticed his frown. He then prodded around the back of the tree and she could see by his face that he had found something.

Lily watched as he pulled some vegetation away, revealing a hole with a metal box inside. He pulled it out and opened it up.

'Alleluia!' Jed whooped, and punched the air with his fist.

There were five bags of gold inside.

Jed took one of the bags and felt how heavy it was. The box itself would weigh quite a bit, so it would be better to discard this and. . . . He looked at Lily's carpetbag hanging from her saddle pommel.

'Oh, I get it!' Lily said. 'I ditch my clothes so you can put the gold in the bag!'

A smile appeared on Jed's lips. 'Not all of them,' he said. 'You can have three of the bags of gold and I'll take the other two. At least you'll be getting all the money back that you spent on financing this little jaunt.'

Jed proceeded to pull out all the bags and handed three of them to Lily.

'I'll put the box back where we found it, then no one will ever know about it.'

Lily nodded in agreement. She pulled the black dress she had worn from Kansas to Denver out. She hoped she would never need it again. Anyhow, she was rich now and could buy all the new dresses she wanted. She pushed it into the hole with the box and covered it with creeper and grass. Her three bags of gold were stowed away with the remainder of her clothes.

Jed put the rest of the jerky and rye bread from the gunny sack in his bedroll and just managed to squeeze the other two bags of gold into the sack.

'Now what?' Lily asked. 'Do we go back to Denver, or go on to Kansas?'

Jed was silent for a while. He knew what he wanted to do, but he could hardly abandon Lily out here on her own.

Lily nodded, realizing the quandary he was in.

'You want to go off in search of Ellie, don't you? You're a fool, Jed! The Indians will kill you. You spent five years in prison because of this gold and now you've got it, you want to go off searching for a woman you hardly know. It will all be a waste of time – and almost surely it will be a waste of your life.'

'I know you're right,' he nodded. 'But I told you before – I've got to do it.'

They decided to make camp for the night where they were, in the small box-canyon. As they ate their frugal meal, both realized how hungry they were and that they could not carry on like this for much longer.

Both were quiet, each thinking the same thoughts. Jed was concerned for Lily's safety and Lily was concerned for her own once Jed rode off after Ellie.

Then their thoughts were broken into by the sound of a horse's hoofs, wheels – and singing.

CHAPTER THIRTEEN

'Who the devil's that?' asked Jed.

'He's religious, by the sound of it,' said Lily.

Within a few minutes the wagon was upon them. A man was still singing lustily and the woman beside him – his wife they surmised – was cradling a baby in her arms. In the back of the wagon were four children, ranging in age from about four to ten, and a man of about forty.

The driver of the wagon stopped singing when he saw Jed and Lily and pulled the horse to a stop.

'Good-evening,' he greeted them.

' 'Evening,' Jed replied.

The woman looked a little afraid.

'Are you going our way, mister?' the man asked. 'If so, we'd be glad of your company along the way.'

Jed looked at Lily before replying.

'My . . . sister here would be glad to join you,

mister. I've got to go in the other direction to check out the relay station that was attacked by Indians. I want to find out if the young woman who helped run the station was killed or abducted.'

The wagon driver nodded. 'We saw the place you're speaking of, mister. We saw two mounds – graves I guess.'

Jed nodded. The coach driver they had met on the way to Denver had already told him about the two dead men. He had obviously buried them before continuing their journey.

'This is a good spot to spend the night. Would you allow us to join you?' the driver asked.

'Sure,' Jed replied. 'Safety in numbers. Although we wouldn't stand much of a chance if we were attacked. Do you carry weapons, mister?'

'We trust in the Lord, my son. The Lord will keep us safe.'

Jed admired his optimism, but the man's faith did not persuade Jed to feel any safer.

The children seemed glad to run about before bedtime. Jed was none too happy when they played around the stunted tree which hid his and Lily's secret. He was glad when they all settled down to sleep.

They were a close-knit family and talked readily about themselves.

'Where are you from?' Jed asked the man. His wife as yet had not spoken. She seemed rather shy and kept herself occupied with the baby.

'Kansas,' he replied. 'I'm a preacher,' he informed Jed and Lily. 'We're on our way to Denver. With everyone there preoccupied with gold, I fear they're in need of the word of God. It is my intention to give it to them.'

'Whether they want to hear it or not?' Lily smiled.

She was given a withering look.

'They have free choice, young lady, but I have to give them the opportunity to hear God's word.'

'I sincerely hope they'll listen to you, Preacher,' said Lily.

Morning came and Mrs Foster prepared breakfast for them all, including Jed and Lily. It was a treat after what they had survived on over the past days.

It was time to leave.

Jed saddled his horse and then Lily's.

'Please don't leave me, Jed,' Lily implored.

'I'll be back,' he told her. 'I'll see you again in Denver.'

'If you bring Ellie back, you won't want to see me any more,' she said quietly, so the others did not hear.

He noted a tear not so far away in her eyes. He wanted to kiss her on the lips, but as he was supposed to be her brother, he kissed her lightly on the cheek.

Jed mounted up.

'Wish me luck, Lily,' he said. Thanking the Reverend and his wife, he waved goodbye and rode off towards the burnt out relay station.

Jed rode for about twenty-five miles until he reached the desolate spot. He noted the two graves without any markers and dismounted beside the burnt-out remains of the station buildings. There was an eerie feeling about the place and Jed gave an involuntary shiver. He knew now, without any shadow of a doubt, that the McIvers killed his parents. If it had been Indians, they would have burnt the place down. The McIvers wanted the place intact for their own use.

Jed walked in among the ashes, looking for Ellie's bones. He pushed debris aside with a foot, examining every inch carefully. There was nothing that even resembled a human bone.

He stood outside and looked around him into the far distance. Where was she? he asked himself. What chance had he of ever finding her?

The place was as silent as the grave. The horses were gone, which was hardly surprising. The horses were most likely the reason for the attack. If only he knew which tribe the Indians came from. The Arapahoes might treat Ellie badly, but if it had been Eagle, her former husband from the Cheyenne who had taken her off, then she would be far safer – he hoped.

Jed filled up his canteen from the trough and allowed his horse to drink from it before setting off once more. He had put the gun he had taken from the McIvers into his bedroll. The chamber only had three bullets in it and he would not stand a chance with the gun if attacked. Maybe if he let the Indians know he was unarmed, they would allow him to approach without firing on him.

After three hours' ride he dismounted to allow his horse a rest. He had noticed tracks of unshod horses mingled with six shod ones leading from the station. It was obvious to Jed that the shod ones were the Indians' prize.

The tracks led to the Smoky Hill River and it was obvious the Indians and the horses had crossed it, heading south.

On the second day of Jed's search he was aware of Indians on the horizon. He carried on towards them. They disappeared from sight but a while later they appeared in front of him as if out of thin air. Jed's heart skipped a beat. Was this the end of the line for him?

He rode towards them slowly and raised a hand in salute. He was surrounded by braves and one took hold of his horse's reins.

'Cheyenne?' Jed asked.

They did not reply.

'Eagle?' was his next query.

They looked from one to another, surprised expressions on their hard features.

A tall warrior came forward on a white horse. Jed noted his rippling muscles and square jaw. Jed had to admit to himself that he was a fine-looking specimen. Could this possibly be Eagle? he wondered.

The brave before him touched his breast with a clenched fist and said, 'Eagle.'

Jed stuck out his right hand as a white man would to another in greeting. He pointed to himself with his left index finger and said, 'Jed. Friend.'

The brave did not take Jed's hand and Jed took it back.

'White man no friend,' said Eagle. His eyes were cold and his lips were set in a firm line.

'Golden Hair,' Jed said, remembering that was the name Eagle had given to Ellie.

Eagle's expression did not alter. Jed did not see even the slightest flicker of emotion cross the brave's face.

'Golden Hair?' Jed asked again.

This time Eagle gave instructions to his braves and two of them pulled at the reins of Jed's horse and led it forward to follow the others who had turned to leave.

Not another word was spoken on the journey to the Indian's camp which was spread along Walnut Creek. There were not many tepees, Jed noticed. It then dawned on him that these Indians were the remnants of the Sand Creek Massacre. How terrible it must have been for Eagle and the others who had been away on that fateful day to return to such carnage. He imagined the grief, anger, and desire for revenge in their hearts.

Jed was pulled unceremoniously from his horse and pushed on to the ground.

An order was given and two of the braves tied his hands behind his back and bound his ankles with leather thongs.

Jed looked up into Eagle's eyes. He tried not to show any fear of the brave. He was sure the more fear he showed, the worse it would be for him. He then pictured the kinds of torture that would be meted out to him. This search for Ellie had all been a waste of time – as Lily had already told him. And now he was to die a slow, painful death.

CHAPTER FOURTEEN

Eagle spoke to his followers in the Cheyenne tongue and Jed was dragged to a mature walnut tree and tied securely to it.

Eagle spoke again and indicated in the direction of the tepees. One of the Indians hurried off, soon to return with Ellie.

Jed saw the surprise, pleasure, then consternation on her face at seeing him there.

'Mr Collins!' she said at last.

Jed remembered this was the name she knew him by. He had promised to tell her his real name when he came back to her at the relay station.

'Hello, Ellie.' Jed tried to give her a smile, but it hardly resembled one.

Eagle spoke to her in his language and Ellie replied likewise.

'Does he intend killing me, Ellie?' Jed asked her. Ellie nodded sadly.

'Is there anything you can do about it?'

'Eagle and the rest of them here hate all white men after Sand Creek,' she explained.

'I can't say that I blame them,' said Jed. 'Tell them that I'm not a soldier and I was miles away in Kansas when that happened.'

Ellie turned to her husband and told him what Jed had just said.

Eagle stepped forward and struck Jed hard across his face.

'Tell him that I always thought the red man was brave. How can he be brave to tie a prisoner up so he cannot defend himself?'

Ellie hesitated a moment before relaying Jed's words.

Jed saw anger flash into the red man's eyes. Being called a coward by a man so securely tied was an insult, but Jed could see that his words had hit home.

Eagle spoke to Ellie again and once more she interpreted his words to Jed.

'Eagle says how brave are *you*? Would you be prepared to fight him for your release?'

'Tell him, yes I would. But also tell him that I want *your* release as well.'

Ellie shook her head and looked quickly up at Eagle. 'I can't leave, Mr Collins. I am Eagle's wife.'

'Wouldn't you leave him for me, Ellie?' Jed asked her.

Ellie did not answer and lowered her eyes.

What was she really thinking? Jed wondered. Was she too afraid to leave – or did she prefer to stay with Eagle?

'How can you stay with him after he killed your father and his helper? Don't you hate him for what he did?'

Ellie did not reply.

Eagle spoke to her again and Ellie told him what Jed had said: that he would be prepared to fight him for his release, but she did not tell him all that Jed had told her.

Eagle gave orders for Jed to be untied. He had already noticed that Jed was not wearing a gun, or a knife. He told one of his warriors to hand over his own knife, which he gave to Jed.

'You must fight for your life now, Mr Collins,' said Ellie.

Jed was not used to using a knife, except for cutting things with. He had never even thought of using one on a man before.

Eagle stood, feet slightly apart, his left arm raised and his right brandishing his knife.

Jed threw his knife away and stood facing the Indian with his bare hands.

He noticed the look of surprise on the red man's face. Was he thinking that Jed was backing down and not wanting to fight?

Eagle became irritated and lunged forward towards him. Jed planned his move, twisting his body slightly as he caught hold of Eagle's right wrist with his own right hand, followed by a knee into his groin and pulling the man over his head, to land on the ground.

Ellie's mouth dropped open in surprise. There were murmurs among the Indians at what had happened. It was obvious that Jed's move had not pleased Eagle.

The Indian got up from the ground. His knife had been knocked out of his hand by his opponent. He looked around for it and Jed took this fraction of a second to plan his second onslaught. He was upon the Indian, grabbing his left arm and once again throwing him to the ground. He waited until Eagle got to his feet once more, then beckoned him with his hand to come to him for more of the same.

Eagle's face was contorted with rage. This white man was making him look foolish and had not, as yet, even hit him. Eagle then put his head down and made a charge at Jed's chest, like a mad bull, but Jed merely turned aside at the last second and pushed him sprawling on to the ground once more.

The Indian looked around again for his knife. One of the onlookers had picked it up and threw it to him.

Eagle was now armed and walked slowly towards Jed, keeping his eyes on his foe all the time. He lashed out with the knife, catching Jed across his left forearm. Blood gushed freely from the wound and Jed took a quick look at it.

The Indian was coming at him again. This time, Jed half turned and, with a flying leap, kicked out at the other man's stomach. Jed heard the other's grunt of pain and surprise. It took only a few seconds for Eagle to come back once more. Jed could tell he was wondering what his next move would be.

The two men circled each other. When at last Eagle made his next move, Jed forced the Indian's arm upwards and punched him hard on the chin. The blow stunned him slightly, and Jed took this opportunity to turn the man around and force the knife from his grip. Jed now had the knife. Both men were now on the ground and Jed had his left arm around Eagle's neck. With his right hand holding the knife he began a downward sweep towards it.

A cry came from the edge of the crowd. It was Ellie's voice.

'No, Mr Collins! Please don't kill him!'

Jed looked across at the distraught Ellie, tears not too far away in her eyes. He got up and allowed Eagle to get to his feet also. Both men stood facing each other. Jed handed Eagle's knife back to him.

'Seems like your wife wants you alive,' said Jed. He knew the Indian did not understand his words, but was sure he would work it out for himself after Ellie's pleading.

Jed held out his hand in friendship to his opponent. Eagle frowned. He did not understand this white man. After a few seconds, Eagle took Jed's hand and they looked into each other's eyes.

Ellie came running up to them.

'Thank you, Mr Collins. Where did you learn to fight like that – or rather, *not* fight?'

'Prison,' Jed answered. 'One of the prisoners taught me. He was taught by a Chinese. They fight like that in China, so he told me. It's a funny name . . . kung fu, I think it's called.'

'Come with me,' she told him. 'I'll see to that cut. It looks pretty bad.'

Eagle walked beside them. He felt bewildered at the outcome of the contest. What would his village think of him? he wondered. Would they think he was weak?

'I must see to my horse,' said Jed. 'He could do with a drink. I could sure use one myself, come to that,' he added.

Ellie spoke to her husband in the Cheyenne tongue. He promptly gave instructions to one of the Indians to see to Jed's mount.

Jed followed Ellie into one of the tepees where she told him to sit down on one of the buffalo robes. She produced some water in a dish and cleaned the wound thoroughly. While she was doing this she told her husband to bring her some moss.

'You attended to a wound once before if I recall,' Jed smiled at her. 'In my shoulder. Five years ago it was.'

'I remember,' Ellie smiled. 'You will keep getting into scrapes, Mr Collins.'

'I said I'd tell you my real name when I came back for you, Ellie.' Their eyes met, then she quickly looked away from his.

'My name's Jed. Jed Stone,' he told her.

'Jed,' she repeated.

'Won't you reconsider coming with me?' Jed asked hopefully.

Ellie sighed. 'Perhaps if you had come for me a bit sooner I would have. But Eagle came back for me first. I didn't think I would ever see him again. We had a child together, Jed, so I am closer to him than I am to you.'

'But do you *love* him?' Jed demanded to know.

After a few seconds she nodded. 'Yes. I do.'

CHAPTER FIFTEEN

Jed was given a meal and some kind of sweetened drink. It tasted like water with honey added. His arm felt sore and throbbed a bit.

After he, Ellie and Eagle had eaten, Ellie took another look at his arm. She poured some honey on the wound and replaced the stagnum moss.

'Ellie, tell Eagle that he and the rest of his tribe aren't safe here. The soldiers need only the slightest excuse to attack – and Indians have given them that excuse by raiding several places recently.'

Ellie interpreted Jed's words to her husband. He looked angry and replied in his own tongue.

'Eagle said the soldiers are on Indian land. It is they who should leave, not the Indian.'

Jed nodded. 'I agree, but that's not how things are. There are more soldiers – armed soldiers – than Indians. They won't be satisfied until all red men are moved on to reservations or killed.'

Ellie spoke again, stumbling as she chose the right words to say in the Cheyenne tongue.

'Someone said in the stage back from Kansas that Canada was taking in tribes and letting them live there in peace. Tell Eagle to take his people there. It's a long journey, but there they would be safe.'

Ellie relayed this to Eagle, who thought about it for a while.

Eagle gave a grunt.

'What did *that* mean?' Jed asked her.

Ellie gave a smile.

'He will give it some consideration,' Ellie said.

Eagle spoke again and Ellie interpreted.

'My husband said, it is time for you to leave.'

Jed nodded. 'I'd hate to outstay my welcome. Does he want me to go right away, or will morning do?'

After a few words between Ellie and Eagle, Ellie said,

'He'd like you to leave now. I'll pack you something to eat for your journey.'

A few moments later Jed was mounted up and Ellie handed him a leather bag of food.

'Your canteen has been filled from the creek,' she told him.

Jed nodded his thanks. 'Goodbye, Ellie. Try and get Eagle to take his people up to Canada.'

'I'll try, Jed. He probably won't listen to me though.'

He rode up the rise and turned in the saddle. She was still there, watching him. He waved his hand and cantered off in the direction of Denver. It would soon be nightfall, and his arm was hurting.

Jed slowed his horse to a walking pace. He looked around him for a suitable spot to make camp for the night. He was on a slight rise and on looking down the slope his heart lurched in his breast. Ahead of him was a long stream of dark blue-coated soldiers. Jed judged there to be about forty or fifty mounted men and they were coming his way.

Jed did not waste a moment and turned his horse's head back towards the way he had just come. He did not know if the soldiers had seen him. He hoped not. His horse started to gallop in the quickening gloom towards Eagle's camp. He had to warn them. Jed guessed the soldiers would camp about where he had last seen them and continue early morning. They seemed to prefer to hit the Indian camps while the inhabitants were still asleep.

Was he being a traitor, warning them? Jed asked himself. After all, the soldiers were white men, like himself, and they were only doing their job, stopping Indian raids on the settlers.

Jed fought a battle within himself as he rode at

breakneck speed towards the village. He would probably get shot by one of the guards of the village for his trouble. But there was Ellie to consider. She could be killed in the massacre and he could not let this happen.

As he reached the edge of the village he called out loudly: 'Eagle! Ellie! Danger!'

His horse skidded to a stop and Jed dismounted, flinging his reins over a bush.

'Eagle! Ellie!' he called as he ran towards their tepee.

Several of the braves pulled back the flaps of their tepees, most carrying rifles or bows. Eagle came outside his own, followed by Ellie who had a buffalo robe wrapped around her.

'Jed, what is it?' Ellie cried in alarm.

'Cavalry – about ten miles north of here. They were about to bivouac for the night in a valley. I rode back straight away. Ellie, you've got to make Eagle and his village leave. Now!' he insisted.

Ellie relayed the information to her husband.

He replied and looked angry.

'Eagle says he will not run from the horse soldiers. He will stay and fight – they all will.'

Jed sighed impatiently.

'Tell him it will be another Sand Creek. Even though you've been warned, you'll still be slaughtered. There are more of them than there are of you. The soldiers are also better armed. If you all leave now, get some miles between you and them, you might stand a better chance.'

Eagle listened to Ellie's words, but he still looked at Jed defiantly. What would be his decision? Jed wondered.

'We will hide,' Eagle said. 'The white men will think we are still inside our tepees and we will attack them. I have spoken.'

When Ellie repeated this to him, Jed shook his head. He couldn't just let the army walk into a trap. If the soldiers got killed, it would be all his fault. If only the Indians would do as he suggested and leave the place now.

Eagle was no fool and guessed what was going on in Jed's mind. Although Jed had warned them, Eagle doubted that he would be able to stand by and not warn the army also. Eagle knew he would have to do something about it.

He called out in Cheyenne and several braves ran up and grabbed Jed by the arms, pinning them behind his back. Eagle gave further orders and Jed felt his wrists being tightly bound.

'Eagle!' Ellie cried. She spoke to her husband. Jed was unable to understand the words, but guessed she was pleading for his life.

More words were spoken and the whole village congregated together. Jed was dragged away and everyone followed, all carrying buffalo robes. The ponies were untied from the line tether and led away from the village.

The Indians seemed to melt into the surrounding land. Just before first light, Jed's mouth was covered with a strip of deer skin, holding his tongue down tightly. There was no way now that he could warn the army that they were riding into an ambush.

The dogs were tied up by the water's edge, and as daylight appeared in the sky, they started barking. They had served their purpose, warning them that intruders were entering the village.

They heard the battle cry from the major as he lifted his sabre into the air.

'Kill them all! Spare no one!'

Jed's blood ran cold as he imagined what would have happened if he had not warned the village of the impending attack.

The soldiers fired into the tepees and slashed the hides that covered the poles with their sabres. It began to dawn on them that by now, some of the Indians would have run out, firing their own weapons.

Eagle gave the order to fire with a downward stroke of his right arm. The Indians stayed where they were, hidden behind a sand dune. They were just the right distance away for their bullets to hit their targets, yet be comparatively safe themselves.

The cavalry were shocked; their horses were being turned in circles of disarray. One by one they fell from their mounts, fatally wounded or dead already. Some noticed where the firing was coming from and charged towards it, only to be shot down before they reached the dunes.

'Circle around them!' came the order, but it was impossible to reach the Indians whichever way they approached.

Jed watched the carnage in front of him. The dogs were barking in alarm, adding to the noise of the gunfire, the horses shrieking as some of them were hit, and the soldiers who were injured and scared witless. It was like a nightmare, one that Jed was afraid he would never wake up from.

A Pawnee scout rode out of gunshot from the fighting. His job had been done in finding the village for his white masters. Now he wanted no part in the fight against the red man.

Eagle saw him edge away. To serve the white man made him a traitor. He deserved to die. He crouched low, making his way around the fighting towards the Pawnee. When he was within gunshot, he fired at the mounted scout. He slumped forward in the saddle, his horse took fright and rode off back the way the cavalry had come. Eagle saw him fall from the saddle.

Ellie watched in horror as she saw that Eagle was now exposed to gunfire, and one of the soldiers was taking aim with his rifle.

'Eagle – get down!' Ellie yelled in Cheyenne.

Eagle was quick to take heed of her warning. He turned and fired at the soldier, who fell from his mount, but not before he himself had received a slight flesh wound in his left arm.

Gunshots were few and far between by now. Horses wandered around, bewildered at not having someone on their backs to tell them where to go next.

Three soldiers remained. All at once there was a loud whoop from the Indians who rushed from their hiding place towards them, firing as they ran.

Two of the blue-coated men fell from their horses, the third, and last remaining soldier, kicked his mount with his spurs and headed away from the scene of death.

Despite his bleeding arm, Eagle ran to the ponies tied to a line hitch and mounted in one leap. He was after the retreating man in an instant.

Now there was no fear of Jed warning the cavalry, Ellie cut Jed's ties and took the gag from his mouth.

'Ellie . . . Just look at it!' Jed said quietly.

The Indians were hard at work scalping every one of the soldiers. They did various other things to them that Jed could not watch.

'It's just like Sand Creek, Jed. Except this time, it was the red man who came out the winner,' Ellie added.

A few minutes later Eagle returned with the

soldier who was riding dejectedly in the saddle. Eagle leapt from his horse and pulled the shaking man to the ground.

'Eagle!' Jed called. 'Enough. You've done enough!'

Ellie did not need to translate Jed's words as she knew that Eagle would understand.

At least the man's death was quick as Eagle's knife sliced across his throat.

The army had paid for the 'battle' at Sand Creek, but Jed knew it had not finished here. There would be many more deaths – on both sides.

CHAPTER SIXTEEN

'We had better bury them,' said Jed, as he surveyed the dead bodies before him.

'Would they have buried us when they had finished? Buzzards, crows, coyote will be well fed on their flesh. It is what they are on the earth for.'

Ellie translated his words.

Jed shook his head.

'How far Canada?' Eagle asked him.

Jed shrugged his shoulders.

'A thousand miles maybe,' he replied. 'If you are all mounted, it should take you about four weeks, depending on the terrain. You have plenty of horses now,' Jed added, indicating the soldiers' mounts.

Ellie was finding it more and more difficult to translate from one language to the other. She had been away from the Cheyenne for nearly two years and had gotten out of the habit of speaking that tongue.

'We will go now,' Eagle decided, and gave instructions to the whole village to pack up everything. The tepees and cooking utensils would be dragged on travois.

As they all set off, Jed made a suggestion:

'It would be better if you sent a scout on ahead, just in case we come across a cavalry troop.'

'Eagle says you insult him. There is already a scout riding on ahead,' said Ellie.

Jed suppressed a smile.

'Tell Eagle I apologize. Insulting him was not my intention. Thank him for banishing me from the village last night. If I had stayed, I would be dead by now, the same as all of them.'

Jed's lightly veiled sarcasm was not lost on Eagle, who grunted when Ellie relayed the message.

'Are you riding with us, Jed?' Ellie asked as they mounted up.

'As far as Smoky Hill Trail. Then I'll head off for Denver.'

Ellie nodded and Jed thought he detected sadness in her eyes. Was she changing her mind about leaving Eagle and going with him? He thought he'd try again and ask her.

'Do you still want to stay with Eagle? It'll be a long ride to Canada, and dangerous. Eagle and his men won last night, but that was only because they were warned. There aren't many fighting men here to hold off soldiers who are waiting for you out in the open.'

She did not reply straight away. He could tell she was fighting a battle within herself.

'I have no one to go back to, Jed. Eagle is my husband.'

'There's me,' Jed said. 'If I didn't want you so badly, I wouldn't have risked my life for you.'

'No. Please don't ask me again.'

Ellie moved away from him and nearer to Eagle.

Jed did not speak to Ellie again for the rest of that day. The Cheyenne were made up mostly of men, with only about five women, plus Ellie. After what she had told him about the Sand Creek massacre, he was surprised even this few still survived. There were no children among the group. There were six dogs, the larger ones pulled a travois containing lighter bundles. They looked more like wolves than dogs and were obviously the offspring of dogs who had mated with wild wolves.

They rode until almost dark, covering about fifty miles, Jed reckoned. Camp was made by one of the tributaries of Smoky Hill River. They did not erect their tepees, but covered themselves with the buffalo robes they had brought with them. Jed noticed Eagle and Ellie were lying close together a few yards away.

As Jed laid out his bedroll and crawled gratefully beneath the blanket, he began to think of Lily. He wondered if she and the religious family had reached Denver safely. He felt rather ashamed of not thinking of her before now, but had to admit that he had had other, more pressing things on his mind. He fervently hoped that they would not come across more cavalry.

The women of the camp set to at daybreak and produced food for them all. As Jed ate, he realized just how hungry he was.

They soon set off once again and Jed noticed one of the braves had ridden ahead of them as a scout.

By midday the scout came riding hell for leather back to the slower party. He did not dismount but spoke to Eagle, gesticulating animatedly with his hand in the direction he had just come.

Jed rode up to them. 'What is it, Eagle?' he asked him.

'Cavalry,' was Eagle's reply.

'How many?' asked Jed.

Ellie translated and told him there were about one hundred men.

Jed's face looked strained.

'Ellie, tell him not to try and attack them. Tell him there is no shame in holding back. To pick a fight with them when it's against the odds is foolish. His people need him. He is no use to them dead.'

Ellie told her husband Jed's words, but Jed could tell he was not convinced.

129

'I will ride out in that direction,' Jed began, indicating right, 'then ride up to them. I could tell them that I saw some Indians in a different direction. When they go, you can all ride on safely without any contact.'

Eagle looked angry. Jed could tell he did not trust him.

'Tell him I wouldn't betray him. I don't want you hurt, Ellie. I'd rather you all didn't come into contact with the cavalry. There doesn't need to be any bloodshed.'

Jed could tell Ellie was putting all her heart into her words, indicating him now and then as she did so.

Eagle looked long and hard at Jed. Then he nodded his head in agreement.

Jed held out his hand and after a moment or two of hesitation, Eagle took it in friendship.

'Send your scout back to watch me, and when the cavalry move off in the direction I tell them, carry on. I'll meet you on Smoky Hill Trail.'

Jed turned to go, then held up his hand to the Indians, giving Ellie one final smile.

He rode hard for an hour then turned his horse in the direction of the oncoming cavalry. After a while he saw them in the distance. Jed kicked his horse's flanks and rode up to them as if in a big hurry.

One of the soldiers rode up to meet Jed, raising

his hand in salute.

Jed appeared breathless as he said, 'Indians! Quite a big bunch of 'em.'

Eagle's scout pulled his mount behind some rocks but kept a lookout. He saw Jed pointing behind him in a direction away from his band of Indians. He nodded to himself. The white man had kept his word. He waited until the cavalry moved off once more towards the place where Jed had told them the band would be. Once the blue-coated soldiers were out of sight, the scout rode back to his band to tell them it was safe to proceed.

Jed carried on towards Smoky Hill Trail where he would wait for the others to catch up with him.

Eagle greeted Little Crow eagerly, and Ellie noticed her husband's relieved face when the two spoke together.

It was around midday when Jed reached the Smoky Hill Trail. He was by the south fork of the Smoky Hill River, a few miles from the burnt-out stage station where Eagle had abducted Ellie for the second time.

He dismounted and allowed his horse to drink while he himself laid on his stomach and drank the cold, clear liquid. He splashed his face all over, leaving him feeling much refreshed. Jed took this opportunity to refill his canteen for the rest of the journey back to Denver.

He took his gun out of his bedroll and examined the chamber. It contained three bullets and he had no more ammunition. Nevertheless, he pushed the gun into the belt of his trousers, giving him a slightly safer feeling.

As Jed sat down with his back against a tree, he began to think about Lily once more. He hoped she had been able to change her three bags of gold into money. He knew she could be a target for robbers as she would be highly conspicuous as a woman in the assay office.

He tore off a mouthful of jerky and chewed on it for a while then tipped his hat over his eyes and fell asleep.

Jed awoke about two hours later with the feeling of something crawling up his right leg. He pushed up the brim of his hat and opened his eyes. Another pair of eyes – small ones – were looking into his.

CHAPTER SEVENTEEN

Jed's first instinct was to jump up and fling the snake away from him. His second instinct was to keep still . . . very, very still, and continue to look the reptile in the eyes. He knew that any sudden move would make it strike, out of fear of him more than anything else.

The next few minutes seemed like an eternity to him. He supposed the snake was considering what kind of creature he was with his face covered in several days' growth of dark hair. The thing it was watching was obviously too big to swallow.

At long last the snake must have thought to itself that it was not worth the trouble to attack the thing beneath it, and slithered off Jed's body and away.

Jed realized that his heartbeats had slowed in panic, and now that the danger had passed, his heart started to beat a little quicker and then normally.

The snake had moved well away from him by now and Jed felt it unnecessary to waste a bullet on it.

He stood up and stretched his arms and looked at the horizon in the direction he had come from earlier. After a few seconds he noticed some movement and within five minutes he could make out the outlines of riders. They were definitely not cavalry, so Jed felt sure they must be Eagle's band of Indians – and Ellie.

He could hardly wait to see her again, but then his emotions dropped at the thought of saying a final farewell.

The Indians arrived at the river about an hour later. Jed was glad to see the expression of pleasure on Ellie's face at seeing him again.

The band rested a while and drank from the river. All too soon Eagle announced it was time to go.

'There are about four forts along the way, Eagle,' Jed told him. 'Keep a watchful eye out all the time, and avoid any contact with the cavalry. Your band is not large enough to fight them all. You'll have to go through Sioux territory also. I hope they will welcome you?'

After Ellie's translation, Eagle nodded. By now he was aware of Jed's wisdom and that he was one white man he could trust.

'Come with us to Canada,' Eagle suggested.

Before he answered Ellie's translation, he looked deeply into her blue eyes, then shook his head.

'Take care, Eagle,' said Jed. 'Take good care of Golden Hair, too. May you live long and have many fine sons.'

Eagle allowed a very rare smile to cross his bronzed features, and nodded.

Jed mounted up and gave them a wave farewell. His eyes rested finally on Ellie and he was sure he detected a tear in the corner of her eye. But was that just wishful thinking on his part?

As Jed's horse splashed through the shallow river, his heart felt heavy. If only they could get word to him if, and when, they reached the safety of Canadian territory. He knew that he would never know their fate.

After about two hours' ride, a stage came up behind him, but did not slow down, forcing Jed to make his horse side-step out of the way. He could hardly blame the driver, for to come across a horseman could mean a hold-up.

As he covered the miles to Denver, he realized just how much he missed Lily's company, which he had enjoyed on the way to the hidden gold. Thinking about her made him urge his mount into a canter so it would lessen the time before he saw her again.

Three days after leaving the Cheyenne and Ellie, Jed rode into Denver. What was his first port of call? he wondered. See to his horse? Find out if Lily was booked into the hotel or change his gold into currency?

On thinking it over, he decided on the three options in that order. Would he need his horse again? Jed wondered. Should he sell it back to the stable owner, or have it looked after until he needed it again? It didn't really matter which, as soon he would have enough money not to even consider either option.

The stable owner looked up from his task of shoeing one of the horses.

'Oh, the Injun-lover back again!' His lips curled in contempt.

'I'll ignore that remark, mister,' replied Jed. 'Do you want to buy this horse back again?'

'Why should I?' he snarled.

Jed shrugged his shoulders dismissively.

'Suit yourself. Just thought I'd give you first option.'

Jed turned his horse's head as if to leave.

'OK, I'll give you what you paid for it – less 10 dollars,' he added.

Jed dismounted and handed the reins to the stable owner as acceptance of the offer.

It was obvious from the man's expression that he had expected Jed to argue the matter, but Jed was in no mood for ill feeling. After what he'd seen and been through lately, all he wanted was a quiet life.

The stable man led Jed's horse into one of the stalls and came back with some dollar bills.

Jed touched his hat to the man, pocketed the money, and walked away.

He took the two steps up to the boardwalk and entered the hotel.

It seemed cooler and darker inside after the glare of the sun outside. He walked up to the reception desk.

'Is Miss Lily Johnson booked in here?' he enquired.

The clerk pulled the large book towards him and used his right index finger to go down the page.

'Sure thing, mister.'

'What's the number of her room?'

The clerk frowned as he looked up at this unkempt, unshaven man.

'Is she expecting you?' he demanded.

'Yeah – at some time or other. What's her number?' Jed demanded.

The clerk considered again for a few seconds before answering.

'Number Seven.'

'Is she in right now?' Jed asked.

'No,' was his curt reply.

Jed nodded, and left the hotel.

Now for the assay office.

Jed's entry into the office had not gone unnoticed. A small, wiry man with more than a week's growth of hair on his face and his hat pulled down low over his eyes watched from across the street as Jed went in and then came out. It was obvious that Jed would be carrying money now. And he intended to relieve him of it.

As Jed walked down the street, the man followed about ten yards behind him.

Jed went into the bathhouse. A slow smile came to the would-be thief's thin lips. He would give his target a while to take off his clothes and get into the water. He imagined how Jed would feel as he luxuriated in the hot water; he would be relaxed – very relaxed and off his guard.

CHAPTER EIGHTEEN

Jed had secreted the bundles of banknotes inside his shirt before he left the assay office. Before taking off any of his clothes he put one bundle inside each of his holey socks, one in each of his trousers pockets and the rest inside his hat. He knew you could never be too sure in a place like Denver, which was full of disreputable characters. A smile came to his face at this thought. He, himself, could hardly be called an upright pillar of the community, as all his worldly wealth he possessed had once been purloined from the stage five years before. However, Jed felt that he had earned it doing five years in the Kansas penitentiary.

As Jed stepped into the hot water and sat down, he felt as if he were in Heaven. All the saddle sores and aches and pains in his joints seemed to gradually melt away. He gave his arm a good wash with the bar of soap. Ellie had done a good job with the honey concoction she had used on the wound and it did not seem infected.

Jed shut his eyes for a few seconds and nearly fell asleep when the bath assistant's voice brought him back to wakefulness.

'Will you be wanting hot water for a shave, mister?'

'Sure. I want the works – a splash of cologne too, if you've got it. I'm meeting a lady and I want to give a good impression.' Jed gave the man a conspiratorial wink.

As the attendant moved away Jed caught sight of someone near his clothes. He was searching hastily for Jed's money.

'Hey, you! Get outa here!' Jed yelled.

The scrawny-looking man had a bundle of the money in his hand and grabbed at another before Jed had time to get out of the bath. The attendant hurried up at the commotion.

'Keep the water! I'll be back,' Jed told him.

He grabbed a towel and wrapped it around his loins, tucking one corner of it into the top at his waist.

The thief was quick. He had got a fair distance before Jed had started to follow.

Smiles, and hoots of laughter came from the assembled crowd at the comical sight of one man running, followed by another with only a towel around his middle.

Jed had longer legs than his quarry, and soon gained on the man. He took a flying leap and pulled him down by his legs and they grappled on the dusty road.

With one mighty blow from Jed's right fist, the small man was laid out cold.

As Jed retrieved his money and stood up, his towel fell away to the ground.

'Jed Stone!' A woman's voice came to him from the edge of the crowd. 'What do you think you're doing, running around Denver with no clothes on?'

Jed hastily grabbed up the towel and wrapped it around himself. As he picked up his money he felt his unshaven face turn crimson with embarrassment. He looked across at the speaker, but knew before he even saw her that it was Lily standing there.

She came up to him, but there was a man with her, and she had her arm in his. Jed remembered that this man had been with the Reverend Foster and his family.

'Have you brought Ellie with you?' she asked, without even asking after him.

'No. She decided to stay with her husband.'

Jed noticed the frown on the man's face. He wondered just how much Lily had told him. They looked very friendly to him – too friendly for Jed's liking.

'What happened to your arm?' she asked, pointing to the wound which was almost healed.

'It's a long story,' he answered with a sigh. 'I'll get cleaned up and meet up with you. Shall we have something to eat at the hotel? I'll tell you everything then.'

She nodded. 'John, here, has been looking after me since we arrived in Denver. He's the Reverend Foster's brother.'

'Thank you for taking care of Lily,' Jed said. 'She'll be fine now that I'm back.'

Lily realized that this was a dismissal, a curt one at that. She was not sure if she minded or not that their brief friendship had now come to an end.

The bathhouse keeper smiled when Jed returned.

'You got your money back then, mister?' he enquired.

'Sure did,' said Jed. 'You can't trust anyone nowadays!'

While Jed had been away retrieving some of his money, the bathhouse man had taken the opportunity of investigating just how much Jed had hidden amongst his clothes. He reckoned it must have been around one thousand dollars or more, plus the amount the thief had taken. He considered peeling off a few dollars, but by the speed of Jed's return with the stolen money, he did not feel like being on the receiving end of one of Jed's fists

– or possibly, a bullet.

After making sure all his money was there, Jed moved his clothes nearer to him this time, then stepped back into the water.

'I could do with some more hot water in here, fella,' Jed told him.

'Right away, mister!'

After a shave, Jed decided he needed fresh clothes before he sat down to a meal with Lily, and half an hour later he came out of the store looking a different man.

As he walked to the hotel he began to consider what would happen next. Would Lily be part of his life? he wondered. Maybe she would prefer to stay with that fellow, John, the Reverend's brother? He would hardly blame her if she did, for he had gone off after Ellie, leaving her with the religious family, and if Ellie had come back with him, Lily would be out of the frame.

What feelings did he have for Lily? he asked himself. Did he want to spend the rest of his life with her? Would she want to spend the rest of her life with him? He decided they would talk, and then maybe things would become clearer.

She was waiting for him in the dining-room when he walked in. He noticed the look of pleasure on her face the moment she saw him. Was this a good sign? he wondered.

'You look smart,' she told him, as he sat opposite

her at one of the tables.

'The best I've felt in years,' he replied, taking her hand across the table.

'What happens now?' asked Lily, searching his grey eyes for some sign of his intentions.

'What would you like to happen, Lily?'

'I don't know, Jed. If you'd come back with Ellie, we wouldn't be having this conversation.'

Jed raised one eyebrow and shrugged his shoulders.

'Who knows. I do know I missed you and I was mighty glad to see you again. That must tell you something.'

'I missed you too, Jed, although I was glad of the Foster family. It would have been scary alone in this town without them.'

Jed nodded his understanding of this.

'What about John? I guess he'd like you to stay with him?'

'Quite possibly,' she answered, hoping Jed would say something to make her give him a more favourable answer.

'Do you think we could make a go of it together, Lily?'

'What exactly are you asking me, Jed? Are we talking marriage here?'

Jed hesitated for a fraction of a second before answering; a fraction too long for Lily.

'If we can get along together on the Smoky Hill

Trail, then I guess we'd be OK if we were married,' was his reply.

'But I'd still be second best to you, Jed.'

The waiter came across and took their order, interrupting their conversation.

Lily noticed that he did not reply to her last words.

The meal had been eaten in comparative silence. Jed told Lily some of what had happened to him since she had seen him last, but not about the massacre of the cavalry at Walnut Creek. He knew that this would always be a part of his life that he could never share with anyone.

As Jed and Lily walked out into the hotel lobby, John Foster stood up from his seat where he had been waiting.

'John!' Lily smiled in greeting.

'I'd like to speak to you, Lily,' he said.

'I'll book myself a room while you talk,' said Jed, and walked off towards the reception desk.

'You and him aren't brother and sister, are you?' John demanded, jerking his thumb in Jed's direction.

Lily did not reply at once and John knew he was right.

'You called him Jed Stone out there in the street, yet you told me your name was Lily Johnson.'

Lily lowered her eyes from his intent gaze. She had hated lying to this man, especially as he was religious, but she couldn't tell him how she and Jed had met up with the sole intention of retrieving some of the stolen gold. She had not even told him that she was now in possession of around three thousand seven hundred and fifty dollars, found at the spot where she and Jed had first met the Foster family.

'Are you and he lovers, Lily?' John demanded.

'No, and that's no lie, I swear to you,' she told him. 'There is no blood tie between us, but we have one thing in common.' She hesitated, wondering if part of the truth would be sufficient for this man. 'Jed's parents, and my father indirectly, were killed by the same men. I'm unable to say more,' she added and hoped John Foster would not press harder.

Foster noticed Jed approaching.

'I guess I'll never get close enough to you now for you to tell me the whole story. I thought you liked me quite a bit, Lily. Obviously I was wrong. You were just using me until he came back.'

Foster strode off out of the hotel without another word and did not look back.

Jed smiled slightly.

'Whatever did you say to him to make him leave like that?' Jed asked her.

'He wanted to know more about us than I was

146

prepared to tell him,' she said.

'You didn't tell him about the gold, did you?'

She shook her head.

'No. The money's in my room. I hope I don't get robbed.'

John Foster marched angrily down the street. His mind was in a turmoil. He had never in his whole forty years felt the way he was feeling at this moment.

Although he had only known Lily for a few days, he was well aware that he was in love with her. She had been friendly and kind to him. He knew he was not much to look at, and had never, ever, had a loving friendship with a woman. His brother's beliefs had curbed any romantic feelings for the opposite sex, and they had never stayed in one place long enough to make any real friends. He thought his day had come at last with Lily, but she had lied to him. Jed Stone was not her brother. But what was he to her – really? He knew he did not stand any chance with her against him, or any other man.

At that moment he found he was walking by a gunsmith's store. He stopped and looked through the window. He had never touched a gun in his life before, yet something inside him was telling him to go inside and buy one.

CHAPTER NINETEEN

Jed spent the rest of that day with Lily in the lobby of the hotel. The more they talked, the more he realized how much she meant to him. He had found her attractive and lovely to look at before, but now he knew just how beautiful she was and that he could not let her go.

Evening came and Lily announced that she was turning in for the night.

'I might have a drink in the saloon before I turn in myself,' he told her.

Lily suddenly felt alarmed at this. Denver was a rough town and she wasn't sure if it had any law. But who was she to tell Jed where he could or could not go. He had not declared his intentions towards her – yet – so he was a free agent to do whatever he wished.

Jed kissed Lily lightly on the lips before she made her way up to her room. He turned towards the door leading to the street.

'You'd better wear a gun, mister,' the clerk called out in warning. 'Things can get a bit dangerous out there at night.'

Jed thought it over for a few seconds, then nodded, acknowledging the man's wisdom with a raised hand, and climbed the stairs to his room. He checked once more that his money was as safe as it could possibly be – tucked between the folds of a newspaper and pushed behind a wardrobe.

He picked up his gun. He knew there were only three bullets in the chamber, but checked it all the same. He was hardly likely to have to kill anyone, and surely not three men.

It was raining when Jed stepped out on to the boardwalk. The street was dark and the flares were only just being lit, some way down. He moved quickly towards the saloon before he got wet and pushed open the batwing doors. He stood just inside and surveyed the room. The last time he had been inside the place was five years ago when he half-heartedly broached the idea of holding up a bank or coach with the McIver brothers so he and his family could pay the mortgage on his home. If they had not been there on that same day, he would never have gotten involved with them and never have robbed the stage. What would his life have been like if none of this had happened? He and his parents would have been evicted from their homestead for a start. And then where would they have gone?

Jed walked up to the bar and ordered a beer. The barman was not the same one who had served him five years ago. He sat down at a small table and looked around him. There was no one he knew, and therefore, no one who would know him, which was good.

A piano was being pounded up in one corner of the smoky room and noisy laughter was coming from another corner as men were involved in light-hearted banter with one of the saloon girls. A fight started with two drunks with no one taking much notice until one of them shot the other. The one still alive ran from the room.

'Billy, go fetch the undertaker!' the barman called to one of the onlookers. 'Another bloody mess for me to clear up!'

Jed noticed that no lawman was called for. He gathered there was no law at this time.

He got up from his seat and left the saloon. He had seen enough 'entertainment' for one night.

The torches were lit by now, but the light from them was uneven, causing shadows. Jed thought he saw a movement on the opposite side of the street, but could not be certain.

He proceeded to walk back to the hotel but a cold, tingling sensation began to run down his back. He was sure someone was following him, with evil intent. Whoever it was was out of luck this time as he only had a few dollars on him.

Jed's hand moved slowly to the gun which was pushed into the belt of his trousers. He turned sharply, his gun in his hand.

A bullet whined past his right ear and Jed caught sight of someone hiding behind one of the wooden posts that held up the awning over the boardwalk.

'Come out and show yourself!' Jed called out. His hand was steady as he held his gun.

A man showed half of his body as he aimed his gun again at Jed. Jed knew he must not miss or he would be killed.

They fired in unison. Neither was a particularly good shot as both were not used to guns, but Jed's bullet found its mark in the other's stomach while his opponent's missed him by inches.

The man staggered and fell from the boardwalk on to the muddy street.

A few men pushed out of the saloon to see what all the commotion was about. Jed crossed the street and bent down next to the lifeless form. He moved the man's head so he could see who he had shot and a gasp escaped him. John Foster!

Foster's gun was still in his hand. Several people came up to have a look.

'It's that feller who goes about with the preacher,' one of the onlookers said.

'So it is!' exclaimed another. 'I wouldn't have thought he'd be using a gun in his line of work.'

'Why did you kill him, mister?' another asked Jed.

'Because he took two shots at me. I didn't even know who he was. He was just a shadow. I've no idea why he would want to kill me.'

Jed felt himself trembling. He had never killed anyone in his life before – except possibly a few Indians who attacked and burnt out his home.

The man called Billy came running up, followed by the undertaker he had been sent to find.

'Another customer for you, Mr Riley,' said one of the gathering crowd.

'Who's paying?' the undertaker asked irritably.

'I'll pay for this man,' Jed told him. 'Where did he live?'

'Mrs Grant's boarding-house up the street aways,' came the reply from one of them.

Jed's heart felt heavy. Now was going to be the worst part of it all – to tell his family what had happened.

He gained entrance to the boarding-house and was shown to one of the rooms off a corridor.

Jed nodded his thanks to Mrs Grant and knocked on the door. The Reverend Foster answered it, dressed in his nightclothes.

His face showed obvious surprise at seeing Jed standing there at such a late hour.

'I'm sorry to have to tell you some bad news, Reverend,' said Jed.

'Please come in. We were in bed,' he added.

Mrs Foster quickly drew on a shawl to cover her nightdress.

'What's happened?' she asked in alarm.

'It's your brother, Reverend,' Jed began slowly.

'John? But he's in his room asleep!'

'Afraid not. More's the pity. He came after me with a gun – fired off two shots. I was forced to fire back, although I didn't know who he was at the time.'

'Nonsense! I don't believe one word of it. John has never used a gun in his whole life!'

'Thomas, look in John's room,' the Reverend's wife suggested.

The preacher went to his brother's door and knocked. He knocked again, calling out his name. After no reply, he went inside. It was dark and he walked over to the lamp by the bed and lit it. John Foster was not there.

'He'll be taken to the undertakers by now,' Jed told him. 'I'll come with you.'

Thomas Foster's face was grim and he stood erect.

'No you will not!' he replied. 'I wish my family had never met you – or Miss Lily Johnson. I blame her for all this. My brother obviously thought he was in love with her. He was a changed man when he came back here and told us that you and she were not brother and sister as you had told us. He thought she felt the same way about him as he did about her. She is nothing but a Jezebel! She led him on only to dash his hopes. Leave now!' he ordered. 'And do not come near us again!'

Jed left the boarding-house and walked disconsolately back to the hotel. John Foster's body had been removed from the street and the piano could still be heard inside the saloon. Life was cheap in Denver.

He hesitated outside Lily's door before knocking. No doubt she would be in bed by now, he reckoned. Perhaps it would be better to tell her what had happened in the morning? He thought about it a bit more, then decided to knock on her door.

'Who is it?' Lily called out.

'Jed.'

He heard her come to the door, obviously taking the time to light the lamp beforehand.

'What's wrong?' she asked, noting the expression on his face.

'Something bad,' he answered.

'Come in!'

She shut the door behind him quickly in case anyone should see him enter.

'You'd better sit down,' she suggested.

'I've just killed someone,' Jed began. He noted the shocked expression on her face. 'It was John Foster.'

Lily sat down quickly on the edge of the bed.

'I don't understand. Why?'

'Someone fired at me from out of the shadows. I turned and saw him about to fire again, so I had to shoot. He missed. I didn't. Lily, I didn't know who I'd shot until I came right up to him.'

Jed could not look her in the eye and hung his head.

'I've just been to tell the Reverend. He blamed it all on you. He said he thought you'd led John on – called you a name.'

'Oh my God!' Lily exclaimed in sadness, surprise and regret. 'I must go to him and tell him how sorry I am.'

Jed shook his head.

'He doesn't want to set eyes on either of us ever again. I reckon we'd better leave Denver as soon as possible. We'll book seats on the next stage.'

CHAPTER TWENTY

Jed pulled his chair nearer to Lily and took both her hands in his. He felt her tremble slightly. She was obviously still in shock over what he had just told her.

'I wish it hadn't happened, Lily. If I hadn't listened to the desk clerk when he advised me to take a gun with me, I probably wouldn't be here right now. I had to shoot back or I'd be dead.'

Lily nodded. 'I understand, Jed. It was all my fault, like the Reverend said. I didn't intend John to fall for me. I just treated him in a friendly way because the Foster family have been kind to me. I was glad of their company after you left me on the trail.'

She sighed and looked down at her lap.

'He obviously read more into the friendship than there really was,' she added.

Jed detected a tear at the corner of her eye and felt sorry for her.

'It'll take a while for me to get over it,' said Jed.

'Jed,' she began tentatively. 'If the Indians hadn't attacked your home, do you think you would have killed the McIvers?'

He pursed his lips. 'It's hard to say for sure. After Ellie told me what Eagle had said to her about them killing my folks, I must confess I considered it.'

'Fate has a habit of stepping in,' she said.

Jed nodded. 'You're right there! If I hadn't been talked into robbing that stage, I would never have met you, Lily.' He squeezed her hands and smiled. 'And do you know something? From now on I don't ever want to leave you.'

He stood up and pulled her to her feet. She relaxed in his arms as he kissed her long and hard. It was an unusual feeling for him as he realized that Lily was the first woman he had ever kissed.

'Jed?'

'Yes, Lily?'

'Would . . . would you think I was too forward if . . . if I asked you to stay with me tonight? Real close to me, I mean.'

A slow smile crossed Jed's face.

'Frightened of the dark again, are you? No, I wouldn't think you were too forward. After all, we're going to spend the rest of our lives together – aren't we?'

Her kisses confirmed it.

Five years later in 1870, Jed was reading a newspaper behind the counter of the general store he and Lily owned. Lily was in the back, attending to their new baby.

'Lily! Come and take a look at this!' he shouted to her.

'What is it, Jed?'

He read a paragraph out to her:

During work on the Kansas Pacific Railway a strongbox was found in a hole along the Smoky Mountain Trail. It was identified as having been stolen from a stagecoach in 1860. The gold it had contained was gone, but a black dress was left in its place.

One of the four robbers was injured in the robbery and served five years in the Kansas Penitentiary without revealing the names of his accomplices.

Could one of them have been a woman?

'The McIvers could never have guessed that a railroad would be laid along that trail when they hid the box,' said Lily. She smiled and returned to her son in the back room as a customer entered.

Ellie came into Jed's mind for a brief moment. 'I wonder what happened to her?' he wondered.